# Say You Won't Let Go

# Also from Corinne Michaels

### The Salvation Series
Beloved
Beholden
Consolation
Conviction
Defenseless

### Return to Me Series
Say You'll Stay
Say You Want Me
Say I'm Yours
Say You Won't Let Go: A Return to Me/Masters and Mercenaries
Novella

### Standalone Novels
We Own Tonight
One Last Time

# Say You Won't Let Go

By Corinne Michaels

## A Return to Me/Masters and Mercenaries Novella

Introduction by Lexi Blake

EVIL EYE
CONCEPTS

Say You Won't Let Go
A Return to Me/Masters and Mercenaries Novella
Copyright 2018 Corinne Michaels
ISBN: 978-1-945920-78-3

Published by Evil Eye Concepts, Incorporated

# An Introduction to the Lexi Blake Crossover Collection

Who doesn't love a crossover? I know that for me there's always been something magical about two fictional words blending and meeting in a totally unexpected way. For years the only medium that has truly done it well and often is comic books. Superman vs. Batman in a fight to the finish. Marvel's Infinite Universe. There's something about two crazy worlds coming together that almost makes them feel more real. Like there's this brilliant universe filled with fictional characters and they can meet and talk, and sometimes they can fall in love.

I'm a geek. I go a little crazy when Thor meets up with Iron Man or The Flash and Arrow team up.

So why wouldn't we do it in Romanceland?

There are ways out there. A writer can write in another author's world, giving you her take on it. There's some brilliant fanfiction out there, but I wanted something different. I wanted to take my time and gradually introduce these characters from other worlds, bring you in slowly so you don't even realize what I'm doing. So you think this is McKay-Taggart, nothing odd here. Except there is...

Over the course of my last three books—Love Another Day, At Your Service, and Nobody Does It Better—I introduced you to five new characters and five new and brilliant worlds. If I've done my job, you'll know and love these characters—sisters from another mister, brothers from another mother.

So grab a glass of wine and welcome to the Lexi Blake Crossover Collection.

Love,

Lexi

# Available now!

# Dedication

To my daughter, Emily: May you always chase your dreams no matter how impossible they may seem. You are beautiful. You are loved. You are special. You are capable of anything.

Sign up for the 1001 Dark Nights Newsletter
and be entered to win a Tiffany Lock necklace.

There's a contest every quarter!

Go to www.1001DarkNights.com for more information.

As a bonus, all subscribers will receive a free copy of
*Discovery Bundle Three*
Featuring stories by
Sidney Bristol, Darcy Burke, T. Gephart
Stacey Kennedy, Adriana Locke
JB Salsbury, and Erika Wilde

"I wish I could turn back the clock. I'd find you sooner and love you longer." — (Unknown)

# Chapter One

"Thank y'all for comin' out tonight!" I step back from the microphone and smile. I love ending a show. It's exhilarating, and as the clapping continues, I wave, basking in the thrill of entertaining.

I was meant to do this.

"Great show, Emily," Matt, the guitarist for Luke, says as I step into the shadows.

"Thanks." I grin. Coming from him, that's a high compliment. "I'm really glad to be on this tour."

Matt touches my arm and squeezes. "We're happy you joined on."

It's been four months of traveling with Luke and his band. His last song went number one on the country music billboards. The fact that he asked me to be on his tour is baffling. I was so lucky he happened to be in the bar that night and heard me sing.

"And she's much prettier to look at than the last guy we had." Luke emerges and hands me a beer.

"Well, thank you." I smile.

"Don't play shy, Emily. You know all the guys around here are happy to have a pretty blonde around."

I roll my eyes and chuckle. As if that matters to me. I'm not stupid enough to ever get involved with anyone from the tour. They call them horror stories for a reason. "Maybe I should dye my hair and get fat."

"Don't you dare." Matt nudges me. "You'll sell more records lookin' like sex on a stick."

I'm not sure if I should laugh or punch someone. "Good to know."

"Don't listen to him." Luke slaps him on the back. "They'll buy your records because of your voice."

I'll believe anything he tells me. My newest song "Don't Call Me Darlin'" is starting to gain traction, which I owe all to Luke. He knows this business, and I couldn't have asked for a better mentor.

Matt laughs. "Comin' from Country Music's Sexiest Man Alive."

"Fuck off, Matt." Luke turns his back to him. "You'll sing the duet tonight?"

"Of course." I smile and try to calm my fluttering nerves and rein in my inner fangirl, which is hard. Sure, he's electric on stage, there is no denying that, but he's also a good guy and never balks at helping his opening acts gain more exposure.

"Good. I'll see you out there in a bit."

The lights shift, and the stage is now set for the main event. Luke drains his beer and grabs his microphone. One day, that'll be me.

I'll be a headliner.

Shortly after I sing the duet and exit the stage, I hear my name being called. Can a woman get two seconds to decompress before the wolves descend?

"Emily?" my manager Ginny calls. "There's a guy who says he knows you and wants to be let back here."

"I don't know anyone from Texas."

She puts the phone up to her ear and grumbles. "He said he's from Bell Buckle and his sister, Priestly, will kick your ass."

"You mean Presley! Cooper is here? Let him back!"

I walk toward the side of the stage where the bouncers are keeping the crowd back. "Emily! Emily!" Two girls yell with their arms raised. I wave and walk over so I can sign the poster they're holding out to me. "You were amazing!"

"Thanks, y'all."

"I agree," Cooper's deep voice says as he comes closer.

"Cooper Townsend, you sly man, showin' up here without callin' me." I wrap my arms around him and hold tight. I have to lift up on my tippy toes just to reach him. He has to be at least six-foot-two where I'm barely five-foot-five. His strong arms close around me, and he squeezes, pulling my feet off the ground for just a second.

He puts me down, and I take a second to look him over. My hands rest on thick muscular arms, his tall frame blocks out the sun that's setting behind him, and I could melt right here. He's always been sexy, but right now, he has that whole tall, dark, and handsome thing going on. The five o'clock shadow only adds to his appeal. The way his hair falls over the dark green eyes that are staring into mine makes it impossible to look away.

"You look great, Em. Really great."

I feel the heat rush to my cheeks, and I duck my head. I'm blushing like a teenager. "Thanks, Coop. What are you doin' all the way down here in Dallas?"

I loop my arm in his, leading him away from prying eyes. "I'm here for a cattle rancher event."

"Ohhh, sounds like a ton of fun." There is a grin on my lips as I tease him.

"They're revealing a few new products and I thought I should be here."

I nod and open the door to the tour bus. "Bein' the sensible rancher you are."

"Of course."

"So, tell me what's new?" We sit on the couch, and I rest my hand on his knee.

Cooper fills me in on all the gossip from back home. He tells me about Grace's little girl, Hannah, and Wyatt and Angie's baby, Felicity. Then he takes out his phone to show me pictures of the girls. Wyatt's little girl is getting so big, and I hate that I haven't met either of those precious babies yet. When he shows me a photo of Trent, Grace, and Hannah, I have to fight back tears. I didn't realize how hard it would be to miss everything since I'm on tour.

"I miss y'all so much. Bein' on the road is tough."

"But you're happy?" Cooper questions.

"I love it. I love singing for people, and Luke Berry is awesome to work with. It's a great honor, and I'm so blessed. I just never thought it would go this far, you know? I thought I'd do like I promised my mama before she died and give it two full years of tryin' to make it before returning back home."

His hand rests on my shoulder. "You were always meant for more." Then Coop leans back with his arm draped across the back. "I'm happy for you, Emmy. I really am. Everyone back home is, too."

I love that he calls me Emmy. No one outside of Bell Buckle ever uses my nickname. It's always Emily or Ms. Young. I just want to be Emmy or Em every now and then.

I lean back against Cooper and rest my head on his chest. "You're such a good guy. I wish I could be back in Tennessee so I could meet Hannah and Felicity."

Cooper's fingers trace up and down my arm. "I wish you were back in Tennessee, too."

"Yeah?" I ask, sitting back up with a smirk.

"Yeah, it's hard not havin' anyone to pick on now that they're all married and havin' babies."

"That's why you wish I was back?" I challenge.

"Well, that and I kind of like you..." Cooper's green eyes turn liquid as he stares at me.

"Just kind of?"

He shrugs, and we both start laughing. "You know how Bell Buckle is. It's the same even when everything changes."

I nod. It really is that way. Some things are meant to be the same, but it's been far too long since I've been home. I haven't had time to visit Mama or anyone else. Grace and Angie both have babies and are always asleep when I finally get around to calling—it's been hard adjusting.

"I can't believe Grace is someone's mama." I laugh as I crisscross my legs.

"It's scary, but she's happy, which is all that matters."

Cooper says the words with so much honesty that I hesitate before asking my next question. However, I'm not known for holding back. I know that he says he's fine with her and Trent, but is he really? It seems crazy to me that after pining for her for years that he'd just be so easygoing about it all.

"And you're okay with her and...him?"

He laughs. "Grace and I were never anything more than friends who shared an awkward kiss. I think I just really liked the idea of her."

"What pretty girl do you have your eyes set on now?"

Cooper's deep green eyes meet mine and they burn. Intensely. I see the heat pooling as his jaw tics just a little before he clears his throat. "The one that I've never quite been able to find."

I'm not sure what that means, and I'm not about to make assumptions, but a bud of hope grows. I've always wondered if we could've been. He has a big heart and a rocking body. I think Grace is freaking insane for not holding on to him. Cooper Townsend is grade A prime meat. One I'd like to sink my teeth into.

"Well." I sigh. "I'm glad you found me tonight."

Cooper looks at the floor and then meets my eyes. "What if I told you I knew you'd be here?"

My teeth grip my bottom lip, and I tilt my head. "Is that what you're tellin' me?"

Our lives aren't the same. He runs a ranch, raising cattle and mending fences, while I'm on the road, singing and following my dream. I have no plans to settle down in Bell Buckle. I'm definitely not a rancher's wife. I'm the girl who was making out with the football players while her best friends were in the 4H club. Hell no. Cooper has never been the guy to end up with a wild child like me.

But we aren't kids anymore.

He leans in closer, and my heart starts to race. "Maybe."

A shiver races from my neck to the base of my spine. No. We definitely are not kids, and there's nothing saying we can't see where this goes.

"Maybe you should make up your mind." I move toward him. Our breaths mingle and heat courses through my veins.

"Maybe I have." His deep voice smolders, causing butterflies to take flight.

"Yeah?" I taunt. "Are you gonna share what you decided?"

His hand lifts with hesitation, but then he cups my cheek. "I'm more of an 'actions speak louder than words' kind of man."

And then, Cooper leans forward, driving me crazy with how slow he moves. Inch by inch, his lips close in.

My breathing grows rapid as the anticipation builds. Years I've wondered. Years I've thought about what kissing him could be like. Crushes are called that for a reason—they'll either crush your heart or crush your self-control. I'm thinking it's going to be the second one with my luck.

I lift my hand and touch his cheek, and then, as our lips are just about to touch, a loud *bang* happens. I shift away as if I just got caught naked by my parents.

"Fuck! You'd think—" My drummer enters and sees the two of us. "Sorry, darlin', didn't know this space was occupied." Vince starts to back out with his hands raised.

My chest rises and falls as I try to catch my breath. "It's fine, Vince.

We were just talking," I say quickly even though it's nowhere close to fine.

"Sure you were." He sniggers.

I hate him.

I glare at him, and he laughs. "I'll be back in twenty minutes. Luke is almost done, and you know he hates hanging around at the venue after the show."

Vince exits, closing the door behind him, and I turn back to Cooper, who looks as if he's trying to control his laughter. "What?"

"Just..." He chuckles.

"Just?"

"Same shit, different girl."

At first, I'm offended. What the hell does that mean? And then it hits me, his kiss with Grace. Well, she and I may have grown up together, and she may be one of my best friends, but we are very different, and I intend to prove it.

I push forward, grip his face in my hands, and press my lips to his.

Within an instant, Cooper's hands are around my waist. He tugs me against him and kisses me roughly. I meld my lips to his and kiss him back with so much passion that I could explode. Our tongues touch, sliding against each other's as I find myself on my back, Cooper over me as my hands roam his taut body.

Jesus. I don't think there's ever been a first kiss that has felt like this.

He pulls back, his eyes searching mine as a smile forms on his delicious lips.

"So?" I ask. "Same shit?"

Cooper's mouth brushes against mine, and he kisses me again. "Not even in the same ballpark."

# Chapter Two

Three loud bangs on the door cause my eyes to fly open. "Emily! Let's go! We're on in thirty minutes," Vince yells in the trailer.

Shit.

I fell asleep.

"Okay! I'm comin'!"

I hop out of bed and start trying to get my face on. I don't love stage makeup, but after seeing photos of the second show without it, I vowed to never look that way again. However, I don't have an hour to really cake it on, so I do the best I can.

Cooper and I ended up hanging out until five in the morning. We spent most of the night just talking, but other parts were spent kissing. I didn't know what I was thinking, but I couldn't keep my hands off him. I tried to nap during the day, but my stomach was in knots thinking about him coming back to the show tonight. I'm on the verge of excitement and complete terror.

"Emily!" Ginny calls. "I'm coming in!"

Ginny is great. She's a force of nature and a little scary, but she's my biggest advocate. She was in Nashville, visiting one of the actors who was filming there, and happened to hear me sing. After the show, she and I spent two hours talking, and I signed with her a few days later. She represents a few big country music names and has her hands in a lot of the entertainment industry. I like knowing I can explore other options if this doesn't work out.

"Hey, Ginny," I reply as I deepen my eyeliner.

"You don't have time for a man," she states without so much as a hello.

"Nice to see you, too." I toss the eyeliner down and dab on concealer.

"I'm serious. There's no time for some random guy."

And to think I was actually starting to like her. I glance over at her and weigh my words. "I don't know what you're talkin' about."

"It's my job to know everything, Emily. I know all about Cooper Townsend and who he is. You're on the verge of becomin' the next Luke. You have to keep your eye on the prize, and boys like that aren't going to keep your focus on the music."

She's nuts if she thinks I'm not focused. She's even more crazy if she thinks that my making out with Cooper one time will end up being more than just that—one time. More than anything, she's lost her ever-loving mind if she believes for one moment that she's going to dictate how I live my life.

"I'm going to pretend that you're drunk," I reply and go back to my makeup.

She means well… I think. And I need to perform in a few. That's what I need to worry about, not her crazy talk.

I feel her bristle and hear her long sigh. "I'm serious. I've seen this a hundred times. Small-town girl gets her big break, only to have a man pull her back home. Telling her that she belongs where she came from. You don't. You belong out there"—She turns and points toward the arena—"on that stage and in the spotlight. I'm telling you, sweetheart, you can't get swept up in some hometown love. He's going to drag you down and crush your dreams."

Anger builds inside me as she says her last words. He isn't like that. Even if we hadn't been friends for over twenty years, after hearing him talk last night, I know that isn't what he would ever do. Cooper spent his life giving up things for people. He isn't going to ask me to do that. And we aren't even anything. We're friends…who happen to like sucking face.

After the initial anger ebbs, it's really almost funny. She knows nothing, and if she's trying to get a rise out of me, she needs to think again. The sound of laughter falls from my lips. "I'm not in love with him. He's a friend, and you have no right to tell me that I can't talk to anyone. I know where I belong."

"I'm protecting you."

"No." I shake my head. "You're protecting your investment. I get it, Gin. I really do. However, I'm a big girl." I glide the red lipstick across my lips and pucker. "And I'll do what I want with whomever I want. Cooper is comin' to the show tonight. He needs to be added to my VIP list and given backstage access." I touch her arm and grab my guitar that sits beside her. "I appreciate it."

I'm not some doe-eyed girl staring at the bright lights anymore. I've spent years doing the grind and somehow making it work. It's never easy, but nothing worth a damn is.

Vince releases a huge sigh as I come to side stage. Everything is all set up for our small opening act. One day I'll get the big lights with crazy props, but for now, we have a few special effects and me center stage.

"Ready?" the production manager asks.

I nod and head out with my hand raised.

This is the moment that I live for. I get in front of the microphone. "How y'all doin', Texas? I can't hear you!" I taunt them a little. The crowd yells, and I smile. "Better, better. Are y'all ready for a good time?" They scream. "I'm Emily Young, and I hope you came to party with us!"

I glance back at Vince, who taps us off.

I start singing our opening number, which is catchy and lighthearted. I like to change our set list every couple of shows and see which the crowd likes more. It seems this one always gets people on their feet. This is also the list that got me bumped to the better position in the lineup. Luke has two bands that open for him. Originally, I was the first, but he found another small band, and I got moved to the coveted second slot. Dreaming about singing for a living usually ends when you wake up not dreaming bigger.

We move through a few more songs, and tonight is one of the best shows I've had so far. Some sing along here and there, but the crowd is alive. They're dancing in their seats or waving their hands, and there's just something driving me to entertain more than normal.

My heart skips a little when I see Cooper front and center. Ginny actually listened. How the hell did she work that fast? I smile and wink as I keep singing, scanning the crowd and doing my best not to look at him again. However, my eyes keep finding their way back to him.

As the show wears down, it's time for my big moment. My favorite part of the show—when I can sing "Don't Call Me Darlin'." It's a deep, soulful song that talks about a woman trying to love a man who doesn't love her back. It's very much based on my best friend Grace. There's something about this song that just calls to me. Knowing you can be hurt at the same time as you're saved. It's full of hope and pain.

The lights go deep blue, and everything is dark. I told Vince and the rest of the band I wanted to sing this one tonight acoustic.

I strum the chords and close my eyes.

"Don't tell me it's too late," I croon.

"I won't give up that easy.

Don't call me darlin' and tell me that you're leavin'.

Don't walk away.

Stop pushing me when you know you want to hold on.

It could be so easy for us, baby.

I've been here, but you don't see me.

Don't let go if you're not ready for me to walk away."

I sing the lyrics from deep inside me, trying to convey the true pain in Grace's heart at the time. I've always believed the best songs are what you know. I may not know pain like that, but when my eyes find a pair of green eyes I spent hours staring into last night, I feel exposed. Suddenly, the song about heartbreak and pain morphs into another meaning.

"Don't let go if you're not ready for me to walk away."

Cooper looks at me, and I sing to him. It's as if no one else is here.

Not the ten thousand other people staring up at me.

No one else exists but us.

This time, the lyrics are about a woman who wants something she probably can't have. It's about a life that might never exist for her, but she wants him even if she shouldn't.

I finish the song, letting the final chord fade as the crowd erupts. My eyes finally move from his, and I do my best to recover. I feel shaken and raw. There is a vulnerability that I've never experienced until just now.

I smile, wave, and give a small bow. "Thank y'all so much!" I move around the stage, grabbing hands with fans. I thank everyone again and raise my hand as I stride off stage.

"Holy shit, Emily!" Vince wraps his arms around me and spins me around. "You were amazing tonight! I've never seen you like that."

"That was nuts! I don't know what came over me." I laugh as he puts me down.

I'm lying. I know exactly what came over me. It was Cooper.

"Well, whatever it was, do that at every show. I think you should sing that song acoustic from now on. I can't believe how fucking intense that was."

Ginny eyes me, and I'm pretty sure she has a guess about what the difference was. She studies me and releases a heavy sigh. "It was a great show, and there were two record producers in the front row. Good night to perform at the top of your game. I'll be sure your friend makes it through security." Ginny turns, takes two steps, and then pivots back. "Wait. Before I forget. This was left for you last night. Probably fan mail that somehow made it backstage. Anyway, it has your name on it." I smile my thanks, tucking the envelope into my guitar case.

I'm on the tour bus, trying to get my stomach to stop flip-flopping. Am I being stupid? After what I felt during that song, I can't see him. Maybe Ginny was right when she said that I'll end up some small-town girl after all. If Cooper is the man who will hold me back, I can't go there. I won't allow myself to end up like my mama. My heart is racing so fast I'm sure it's going to fly out of my chest. When the hell did that song become anything about me? Ugh. I'm not answering the door when he comes.

Nope.

I'll just ignore it, shut the lights off, and hide.

Trying to calm my nerves, I pace. My eyes catch on the letter that Ginny gave me, which is still tucked inside my guitar case, and I pull it out. It's surreal getting notes from people gushing over me. I've only really been touring for a few months. I don't know how to take it. It's an amazing feeling. I tear the flap open and pull out the single sheet of paper before unfolding it. Then, I gasp, dropping the letter to the ground.

*What on earth?*

I pick it back up with a trembling hand. A collage of pictures of me from various shows and online blogs are arranged haphazardly. As if that wasn't creepy enough, the words, "You're my darlin'" are emblazoned in the middle. There are several pictures of Luke and me, and Luke's eyes have been scratched out. The whole thing is disturbing to say the least. This would be a first for me.

I'm staring at this crazy collage, wondering what in the world is wrong with people. Who would send this to me? Why? I'm a nobody, and really it's crazy that people have time to do this. This person needs a hobby, that's for damn sure. I look closer, trying to figure out what concert it was taken at when a knock on the trailer causes me to jump.

"Em?" Cooper's deep voice filters through the room. "You here?"

I toss the crazy person letter under my lyrics book and chew on my thumbnail.

"Emmy? I see the lights on."

Damn it.

My mind goes back to the concert and how fast he made my heart race. How him just being there made the song come to life inside me. Maybe this is a mistake, but I worry the bigger one is running away from him.

I stand and move to the door.

"I'm here," I say with the metal shielding me from his eyes.

Instead of making me want to cower, the sound of his voice causes me to react completely different and irrational. I open the door and rush toward him, wrap my arms around his neck, and press my lips to his. I kiss him like I need it. And I do. I want nothing more than to feel him because it feels like the right thing—the only thing—I should do. I feel safe in Cooper's arms.

His hands grip my legs, and he hoists me into his arms while I kiss him deeply. My tongue slides against his, and I moan in his mouth.

Cooper walks with me wrapped around him. He holds me to his body, and I feel all the emotion pouring out of him. The moment we shared while I was on stage was just as intense for him as well. He moves to the back bedroom and lays me on the bed. His fingers lace in my hair and he takes control, moving his mouth against mine as he drinks me in, slowing the kiss until his lips are a feather-light brush against mine.

"Hi." He breathes the word.

"Hi." My cheeks burn as I realize I assaulted him without even saying a word. "Coop, I don't know what that was—"

He presses his finger to my lips. "Don't say anything."

"But," I mumble, and he shakes his head.

I want to tell him about the letter and how scared I am, but at the same time, I don't want some bizarre fan mail, which is probably nothing, to ruin our night together. Cooper is protective. If he knew that I got a letter like that, he'd probably force me to report it. Tonight, I just want him without the crazy that my life is turning into.

"You leave for Houston tomorrow, and I'm going back to Bell Buckle a few days after that. It doesn't have to be any more complicated than that."

I wish that were true. Cooper isn't some guy I found on tour—he's a friend. We grew up together, and our lives are very intertwined. It's clear we both are feeling this, and I don't want this to be the end. I want passionate nights and days spent getting to know each other more. I want whoever sent me the letter to never contact me again.

I'm a damn fool.

Wanting more with Cooper isn't possible. I'm on tour for another month, and then who knows what after that? As for the letter, I can't control crazy fans. I can only hope it is a one-time thing.

Cooper's eyes hold mine. "I'm not askin' for anything, Em. I'm just sayin' we should enjoy tonight. Okay?"

I nod, and he removes his hand. "My tour is over soon." I touch his jaw.

"And you know where I'll be."

"You think I should come find you?" I say with a teasing tone.

"I really hope you do."

"We'll see." I shrug, and he laughs so hard it shakes the bed.

Cooper rolls to his side, pulling me with him so we are face to face. "You know that there are girls lining up for a chance with me."

I raise a brow and snort. "In Bell Buckle?"

"And the area surrounding."

I smother my laughter and roll my eyes. If I wasn't from the area, he might've sold me, but there's no line of girls anywhere in Bedford County, Tennessee. On the other hand, if I lived there, I'd be first in the Cooper line.

He's definitely the most eligible bachelor in a town of a hundred people.

I grin as I touch his face. "Well, lucky for me that you aren't home to get all the attention of those women. I mean, I feel like I should thank my lucky stars."

"Oh, you should."

"Whatever will I do when you leave?" I ask playfully. "How will I get through the nights, wonderin' if some girl has stolen your heart?"

I'm partially joking, but there's an element of truth to that. Not because he's mine or I have any claim, but I wonder if he has someone in line back home. I wouldn't blame him.

Cooper brushes my hair back off my cheek. "Jealous?"

I shake my head and scoff. "No."

"Really?"

"Not even a little. I've seen your pickins… I'm not worried."

He grins. "Oh, so you're sayin' you're my best option?"

I sit up quickly and shift to my knees. "Who said I was an option?"

Cooper follows the motion and shifts forward. His nose rubs the side of mine, and I shiver. "Are you?"

"What if I am?"

He leans back, giving me an open look into his heart. "Then you'd get a pass to the front of the line."

"I'll let you know tomorrow if I want that pass or not."

Cooper grins and sits back. "Challenge accepted."

# Chapter Three

"Good morning," Cooper's deep voice grumbles against my neck.

"Hi there, cowboy," I reply, nestling into his body a little deeper. "Sleep good?"

I did. We passed out at some point during the night—fully dressed. I've never had so much fun doing nothing before. All we did was talk about everything and anything, and of course, I kissed him—a lot. How could I not? Kissing Cooper feels like coming home. It was full of anticipation, joy, and a feeling of safety that I could just fall if I had to. Cooper was there to catch me all night.

His nose rubs up and down the back of my neck. "I did," he replies.

His arm snakes around me, tightening and holding me secure. I try to remember that I need to keep myself in check. Yes, this is Cooper Townsend, but at the same time, we live worlds apart. It isn't smart to get caught up in something that won't ever be anything more than just this.

Feelings lead to heartbreak. Heartbreak isn't something I can afford right now.

"What time does the bus leave?"

I flip over to my other side so I can look at him. "Not until tonight. Luke likes to travel at night and see the city we're in during the day. So, I have all day. Why?"

He smiles while resting his hand on my hip. "Spend the day with me."

"Coop." I sigh. We had talked about this last night. That we'd say goodbye in the morning and keep things light. No complications. No promises. Not until the tour was over and I was back in Tennessee.

Then, who knows, but I'm all too aware of how easy it would be for me.

"It's breakfast, lunch, and dinner. Just a day of us hanging out," he presses.

My eyes narrow slightly, and I pull my lips to the side. "I don't know. We agreed…"

"Emmy, we have a very looming expiration date. I'm just askin' my friend to hang out. Besides, what other options do you have?"

I roll onto my back and put my elbow over my eyes. In all honesty, I want to spend the day with him. I want to spend as much time as I can with him. Maybe this will quench a little of my thirst for the man next to me.

Maybe.

"All right, fine. We'll go see Dallas together."

He climbs on top of me, giving me a sweet kiss on my lips. "I knew you'd cave. You can't resist me. I'm wearin' you down."

My hand slaps his arm, and I shove him off me. "Yeah, right." I laugh. "I need to shower. Go get yourself ready, and I'll meet you in an hour." I hop off the bed and open the door to the bathroom.

"Need help?" he offers.

I turn my head quickly, tossing my blonde hair over my shoulder and grinning. "You wish, Cooper Townsend. You wish. You best be goin', time is tickin'."

\* \* \* \*

An hour later, I'm outside Cooper's hotel with a roadie's car that I borrowed. I know exactly where I'm taking him today.

Cooper comes out, wearing a tight pair of jeans and a flannel shirt with the sleeves rolled up. Dear Lord, he looks good. His wet hair looks almost black, and the green from the shirt makes his eyes look even more emerald. It should be illegal to look so sinful.

"Darlin', you need to go back and change," Cooper says as he looks me up and down.

"What?" I glance at my outfit, completely baffled by what the issue is. I'm wearing a jean skirt, white tank top, and an off the shoulder floral cover. I look cute.

"I'm not lookin' to fight anyone while I'm here."

He walks straight to me and pulls me into his arms. "Fight?"

"Every single man is going to try to get to you, Emily. I'm goin' to be a busy man fending them off."

My hand touches his chest, and I smile. "I think you're big enough to take them all."

"You think so?" he teases.

"Well, if you aren't, it'll be fun to watch you try."

He laughs and leans in for a kiss. To any passerby, we probably look like a real couple, and a small part of me wants to run. I know the real way this will turn out. It won't be smiles and hugs. It'll be yelling and disappointment because I won't give up my life and neither should he.

I'm getting so far ahead of myself.

For all I know, Cooper just wants to get laid and be done with whatever this is between us. That would be great to delude myself with, but I don't believe that's the case.

"What's on the agenda?" Cooper asks, pulling me away from my doom and gloom thoughts.

"Oh, you're going to love it."

He laughs. "I'm sure I will, but I'm a little scared."

I hook my arm in his, and we head down the street. It's only a few blocks away. Neither of us says much as we stroll along. It's a beautiful day. The sun shines through the clouds providing a shadow.

"Scared of me?"

"Weren't you the one who organized putting food dye in the shower heads?"

I'd almost forgotten about that. Each year, the boys would prank the girls right before homecoming. It was always something lame and never actually did any damage, but there was no way I was letting them get the edge on us. Presley, Grace, and I snuck into the boys' locker room with medicine capsules filled with food dye. Once they were in there, it was like a ticking time bomb.

Whoever turned the shower on when the capsule melted enough was going to get a surprise.

Of course, the poor kid who turned red wasn't our target, but it stopped them from even attempting anything that year.

"Whatever do you mean?" I feign innocence.

Cooper laughs and jerks his arm out, causing me to sway. "I know better. Presley got double the barn duties that month. I know you all were behind that mess."

I grip his thick arm a little tighter. "It was meant for Zach and Wyatt. Those bastards always got us. I did feel bad for Mason. He didn't deserve to be red for a week."

"His mama was mad."

I giggle. "Oh, I know."

We walk a little farther, and I start to get excited. I've never been here, but I thought the irony was just too perfect to pass up.

We make it to the entrance of Pioneer Plaza, and Cooper bursts out laughing.

In front of us are hundreds of cattle sculptures. They line the park and walkways, cutting through the water and grass as we enter.

"This is incredible."

I look up and smile. "A little of you is right here in Texas. Cows and all."

Cooper throws his arm around my shoulders, tucking me against his side. "Look!" He points over to the sculpture of the cowboy riding alongside the roaming cow.

"It's you!"

He kisses the top of my head. "I don't wear chaps."

"You could totally pull them off." I joke, sort of.

"Not since my rodeo days."

My hand runs down from his chest over the hard planes of his abs. "I think you should try them on the next time you move the cattle. I bet your ass would look mighty fine in some chaps."

His eyes glimmer with amusement. "Only if you agree to ride with me."

"Do you remember me ever riding a horse?"

So not my thing. My parents weren't in the same crowd as the Townsends, Henningtons, and Rooneys. My father was the town drunk, and Mama was always making excuses for him and doing God knows what with other men. Daddy tried to quit once, but then he lost his job at the stables. Instead of going out and finding another job, he decided to drink more and sleep all day. My childhood was the opposite of my friends.

I didn't have nights at the creek or long horseback rides. I had driving to the bar, helping Daddy in the car, and then going to pick up Mama from waitressing three towns over. Not to mention the fact that

Rhett Hennington gave me a job at night cleaning stables so we could afford to eat. There was never any money for a horse in my life.

Sad little poor girl with the crumbling house and a drunk for a father.

No one ever said it to me, but I was side eyed a lot.

"You know, I don't remember all that much about you as a kid." Cooper looks off and rubs his chin. "I know you were around, and we talked, but you never spent the night at the house, did you?"

"There were never many sleepovers in my childhood. I didn't spend all that much time around your house especially. Grace and I hung out here and there, but it wasn't until after my daddy passed away that I started hanging out with Presley more."

A frown forms on his lips, and I have a feeling he's remembering why now. "I forgot about that. I'm real sorry 'bout your dad."

"I'm not," I say with no hesitation. "Good riddance."

Cooper looks down with surprise.

"Don't get me wrong, I loved my daddy just fine, but he didn't make life easy on me or my mama. I didn't enjoy workin' at night on the farms just so we didn't have the electric shut off."

"I never knew." He stops walking and puts his arms around my hips. "Why didn't any of us know?"

"I never wanted you to."

I became a professional at hiding things. I was lucky I had Grace and Cooper's sister Presley as my friends. They would pass me clothes so I didn't have to wear the tattered jeans and shirts that were falling apart. Since Grace was always in pageants, she was slipping me makeup and beauty products. I never *looked* poor, but I was.

"It wouldn't have mattered."

"No?" I challenge him. "I never had friends sleep over. Your mama and Grace's wouldn't let them. I didn't have boyfriends because I wasn't going to bring them home to meet my daddy, who probably would've been passed out anyway. I had Pres and Grace, but my best friend was my guitar and my notebook."

Music was the only way I could breathe. I wrote songs, learned how to play guitar, and sang my heartbreak out of my soul.

"We didn't have money like you think." Cooper tries to soften whatever hurt he saw on my face.

"Coop." I touch his chest. "We weren't just not-makin'-ends-meet kind of poor. We were getting bags of food from the Rooneys so I didn't starve. I was shoveling shit at night after all the farmhands went home at the Hennington Horse Farm without anyone knowin'. I'm just a poor girl from a small town in Tennessee. It was the way my life was, and it was nothing like what you remember."

Cooper's eyes fill with a mix of sadness and awe. "And look where you are today."

The awe wins out.

His head dips, and his lips touch mine. When he pulls back, a small smile paints his face. "When I look at you, I don't remember that. I just see the strong, beautiful girl that I can't seem to look away from. I see long blonde hair, big blue eyes, and the sexiest woman I know. I see a girl who came from a going-nowhere town and is takin' the music world by storm. You're not your past. You're not what you remember either."

My pulse quickens, and tears pool in my eyes. He has no idea how much what he just said means to me. I can't stop myself even if I wanted to.

I have to kiss him.

I lean up on my toes, grip his head, and kiss him right in the middle of this park. I hold him to me, thanking him, needing him, wanting him with everything inside me. I've struggled my whole life with not thinking I was good enough for my friends. I wondered if any man would ever see past the trailer park and rumors of my family.

When I pull back, Cooper grins. "What was that for?"

"Bein' you."

His hands glide up my back to tangle in my hair before he dips me low, pressing his mouth to mine. Cooper's tongue glides against my lips, and I open to him. He kisses me hard and ardently.

"Whooo hoo!" We hear people calling around us. "Hell yeah! Kiss her, man!"

I turn my head and tuck against his chest with a giggle.

Clapping and cheering happens from passersby.

Cooper laughs and finally straightens, pulling me back up with him.

"I'm so embarrassed," I admit.

He leans back and shakes his head. "I'm not. I've waited a long time to feel this way. To not give a shit about kissin' a girl in the middle of wherever we are. To want nothing but to wrap my arms around her any chance I get. I've waited a long time for you, Emily. I'm not sure I'll be able to let you go."

Fuck, fuck, fuck.

I don't want to lie and tell him I don't feel exactly the same, but I can't say the truth either. Not yet.

I release a nervous laugh that I try to play off as cute. "Oh, umm," I stammer. "You're makin' me blush."

Cooper's smile falls, but he recovers quickly. His arm goes back around my shoulders, and we start to walk again. I try not to hear his words echo in my head, but I fail. I know this isn't a typical boy-meets-girl situation. There's history and a very established friendship, but I've never been tied down. That's what has made this so easy. The traveling, recording, playing night after night in a bar. Being single has allowed me this life.

I hate that I ruined what has been a really great morning. I need to fix it because Cooper doesn't deserve it.

I pull him over to the bench, and we sit. "I'm sorry," I say with his hand in mine. "I got weird, and you don't deserve that. It's just that I like you. I've always liked you, but now, it's different. I liked you in Bell Buckle, but we weren't makin' out in the center of town. It's different, and we're in two really different places—and states," I tack on.

"I'm not tryin' to push you, but we're not gettin' any younger. I don't want to look back on my life and wish anymore."

Cooper runs his thumb across the top of my hand, and I look off at the bronze cattle in front of us. "That's your life, Coop. The farm, the family, Tennessee, but it's not mine anymore. My life is music and traveling. I don't know how long I'll make it in this business. I'm not young and fresh. I can't give you all my heart. Not now. Not when I'm living on borrowed time in the music industry."

He leans back and grins. "Well, I'll just have to wait."

"Wait?"

"Here's the thing…" He moves close, giving me a glimpse into his heart. "I know what we have isn't just one sided. I know what that looks like." Cooper pauses, and I know he means with Grace. "You like me more than you want to. You like kissin' me and touchin' me, and we both know this is more than either of us is ready for. I've got the farm and you've got your music, but why the hell does that mean we can't have each other? Who says you have to live in Bell Buckle for us to work? Who says you have to give up your career? Who says I have to?

Why have you already decided a future that neither of us can see? So"—Cooper lifts my chin, forcing me to look him in the eye—"are you willing to wait?"

My heart slams against my chest and my hands tingle. How has this happened to me so quickly? How has just two nights of being with him caused me to feel so much? It's crazy and way too fast and so…right.

"For how long? How long are you willing to wait?"

He shakes his head, and his eyes are full of hope. "I don't have the answer to that. I know that I'm willing to do what I can. Are you?"

It's not as if I've never wanted a man; I just wanted the right man. I saw no reason to waste my time on silly crushes because nothing was worth it. Now I'm sitting here with him and it feels like everything is new. The sun is brighter, the sky is bluer, and the world is more exciting because I'm seeing it for the first time.

The words fall from my lips as my skin prickles. "I'll wait. It's only a month, and then, when I'm back in Tennessee, we can see what this is."

Cooper's fingers touch my cheek, and he slides his hand back, cupping my face. "A few weeks and then you'll fall in love with me."

If he only knew how I felt already. Last year, when he and Grace were no longer a possibility, I felt something. I thought it would go away, but it clearly hasn't. Instead, it's grown stronger than I ever imagined. There won't be weeks. I'm pretty sure I'm already in love with him.

# Chapter Four

My day with Cooper is magical. We spend it doing all kinds of tourist things like having lunch at the most amazing barbeque place and then standing on the grassy knoll where the alleged John F. Kennedy killer stood. Everything is perfect, and there isn't any more talk about what we could be or what we already are, just light and fun.

Until the sun starts to fall.

Then we know that the time we're enjoying is drifting away from us. When the sky moves from beautiful purples and blues to black, our spell is broken.

"I should get back," I say with my forehead resting against his.

"You don't want them to leave without you," he agrees.

Don't I? I don't want to leave Cooper.

Which is fucking stupid and exactly what I am trying to avoid being.

My fingers grip the sides of his flannel shirt, and I tug. "I don't want to go."

He cups my face, waiting until my eyes meet his. "I don't want you to either, but you have a music world to conquer, and I've got an expo that I skipped out on today."

"Always the responsible one." I rib him.

"Not at all. If I could have my way, we'd be up in my room right now. I'd be kissin' you and convincin' you to stay with me."

My lips part, and I think about how much I want that. I want him—so much. "Coop."

"But it's not right and not what I promised you."

I nod. "I hate bein' right."

Cooper laughs and brings his lips to mine. "Go. Before I change my mind and lock you in my room."

I raise my brow and grin. He chuckles again, and this time, I lean up and kiss him hard, hoping to convey just how much I don't want to leave. I would happily stay with him, learning more about the man who is quickly stealing my heart.

Damn adult responsibilities.

"Is it crazy that I miss you and I haven't even left?" I ask and instantly wish I hadn't.

He's been open and honest, though. He's told me clearly how he feels, and as much as I hate being vulnerable, it's just true. The fact that tomorrow I won't see him makes me sad.

"I think it would be crazy if you didn't miss me. I've been told that I'm a catch."

I roll my eyes and grin. "Yes, I guess you're lucky I'm so good at fishin'."

Cooper looks down at his watch and groans. "You gotta go, darlin'."

Darlin'.

I've heard it my whole life. Daddy called Mama that, Zach called Presley it, and Lord knows, Southern boys love saying it when they're trying to blow a girl's skirt up. When Cooper says it like that, though, I could cry. Two syllables laced with so much emotion that it forces the word to take on a new meaning.

It's a song and a prayer.

It's a promise filled with hope.

It's a sign of something more between two old friends.

If I don't walk away now, I won't go. My feet move back, and my fingers hold the fabric, letting it slip from their grasp. "I'll call you."

He smiles. "I'll be here."

I move backward. "Go learn about cows and shit."

Cooper shakes his head. "I'll do my best."

"I'll see you soon."

"I'm countin' on it."

I turn my back and get in my car as he stands there with his hand up. I touch the window and smile. "Bye, Coop," I say, and he winks.

My phone dings with a text from Vince, and I know I can't wait any longer. I have to go. Putting the car in drive, I try not to look at him, and I move forward, leaving Cooper in the rearview mirror.

* * * *

The bus is parked in the new arena in Houston. We had an issue with Luke's bus and ended up not leaving Dallas until two in the morning, but I slept restlessly the four hours it took us to get here, wishing I were with Cooper. If I don't get more rest, I'm going to be a bear for the show. I toss and turn for another thirty minutes before there's a knock on the door.

Ginny steps in without invitation, saying, "I saw your light on."

"Yeah, I can't sleep."

She moves to the couch, and I rub my eyes. "I'm heading to Nashville in ten minutes. I wanted to check in and see what the plan is when you're finished with the tour in a month?"

I'm not sure what to say. Before Cooper showing up here, the answer would have been easy—go back to Nashville and bust my ass. Now, I want to maybe visit Bell Buckle a bit. I haven't seen Grace, Presley, or Angie for a while now. It would be good to catch up.

*Sure, Em, that's the reason.*

I can't even lie to myself.

I've learned a lot about Ginny, and the thing I know more than anything is that she likes honesty. That's what I'll give her. "I think I'm going to take a few weeks in Bell Buckle. Then I'll head back to Nashville."

Ginny doesn't speak, she just nods slowly. Great. I'm now "that" artist. The one who says she wants it all and then falls for some guy and throws it away.

"So, two weeks there?" she asks.

I'm not sure I can endure more than that in Bell Buckle, and that should be enough time to figure out what I'm feeling. "Yes. No more than two weeks."

She stands, sighs, and then hands me a stack of envelopes. "You got another batch of mail. I know you still refuse to allow my team to handle them for you."

I smile. "Fan mail is something I've dreamed of," I explain. "Not everyone is as fortunate as I am. I like to stay humble."

Ginny rolls her eyes with a grin. "I'll see you in Nashville in a few weeks."

"Yes, you will."

When she leaves, I grab the stack of notes and start going through them. My process with this is simple: I read them and then keep the addresses to send a custom fan club guitar pick. Sometimes, depending on the letters, I'll write back. It's cathartic for me on some level.

I open the next letter and smile. A little seven-year-old who saw the show in Phoenix and says I'm her new favorite singer. This is why I open them all. I write her back and make a note to include a few things.

The next letter has no return address. I hate when they do that.

As I pull the note out, a chill runs down my spine.

The letter is cut out newspaper letters that spell out: You should be mine.

*What the fuck?*

This is getting ridiculous. Nothing is threatening in this, but what is wrong with people? Do they have nothing better to do? Plus, I'm not even a little bit of a big deal. I'm a baby in this industry.

The last thing I want to do is cause waves on this tour, either. I need to be smart and not end up labeled as a problem child who cried over a few stupid letters. Luke told me yesterday about a fan who sends him a letter a day.

This is what being in the public eye means and I need to get used to it.

I huff out a breath and toss the letter aside.

No more fan mail for me right now.

My head is filled with so much emotion that maybe writing songs is what I should do.

I play a few melodies, and one starts to take hold. Words pour out as I start to arrange the notes.

Words about maybe finding something I didn't know I wanted, worrying about if things don't work out, and then learning to accept the fear.

I sing and strum my guitar, stopping randomly to jot things down.

Lost in the process, I almost don't check my phone when it pings. Almost.

*Grace: So, do I need to buy a ticket to talk to my best friend?*

*Me: I know someone who could hook you up.*

*Grace: I miss you.*

Instead of texting back and forth, I dial her number.

"Hey!" She answers on the second ring, and I can almost hear her smile through the phone.

"I miss you more!"

"Not possible," Grace disagrees. "How are you? How's the tour?"

I fill her in on the fun stuff she loves hearing about. It's a regular soap opera on tour. People hooking up, some married, and lots of crazy drinking. I'm lucky that I've been able to stay out of all of it. We laugh about some of the cool places I've gotten to see. Grace is a history nut and loves tourist stuff. I sent her a few photos when we played in Gettysburg and visited the battlefield.

Now I need to tell her what I've been slightly nervous to say. "There's not really much to say, I've been getting weird letters, but that's par for the course." I brush that part off and release a shaky breath.

Grace clears her throat. "What do you mean par for the course?"

I should've kept my mouth shut. "It's normal for artists to get weird fan mail. Luke was telling me about some of the stuff he's gotten. That's not what I'm nervous about, Grace."

"Trent!" Grace calls, and I drop my head back. "Emily is getting letters that she said are weird."

"Grace!" I yell in the receiver. "It's really not a big deal!"

"You're all freaked out." She huffs. "I can hear it in your voice. Don't lie to me, Emily."

She's sweet to care, but that isn't what has me feeling this way. "I'm nervous because I need to tell you that I saw Cooper when we were in Dallas."

"Really?" Her voice goes an octave higher and shifts to excitement. "I know he's out of town, but I didn't know he was near you."

"Yeah, and..." I pause, trying to get my courage. "Well, we...we...we kind of hooked up or I don't know."

"Oh my God!" Grace screeches. "She's fine, Trent. Go away." She yells and then covers the phone.

I can hear her yelling at him and telling him to leave her be, which makes me giggle. They're so funny together.

"Sorry, he thought something happened with these letters. *So*, how was it? Do you think there's somethin' there? Are you guys, like, together? Oh, Emmy! Spill it! I need details. Ahh, I'm so happy!"

She really is. There's no weirdness, not that there really should be since all they've ever shared was one really bad kiss. Still, I don't know... There's something about dating your friend's ex that feels like betrayal. Even though Grace knows how I've felt about him for a year now. One night when I was visiting Mama, I got shitfaced and spilled how I really felt about Cooper to Grace and Presley, who were overjoyed. Grace insisted that Coop felt the same but was too afraid I'd turn him down. Funny that we were both worried about the same thing.

When I saw him, it was like all the tension that I thought I had dissipated came roaring back.

Only it didn't just bubble, it boiled over.

I flop back on the bed and blow a long breath out. "I don't know what we are. But he was in Dallas and came to the show. He came back to the bus, and it just happened. Then we spent the whole day together again, and I can't explain it."

"Did you sleep with him?"

I wish. "No, we spent two nights talkin' and makin' out. And then we explored Dallas. It was crazy, Grace. It's nuts that I spent all night thinking of him, wishin' he was with me. It's insane that I want to get a car and drive back to Dallas, right?"

"What do you think?" Grace answers a question with a question.

I hate that.

I groan. "I think a year's worth of squashing feelings has just been let out. The sparks between us were instant, and being with him was so easy. It is truly the way you describe bein' with Trent."

"If it's easy, then it's right. You've liked him for a while. And I know he's liked you for just as long. I guess the question is, what are you going to do about it?"

"I don't know."

Grace huffs. "You know, if I remember correctly, you're the one who told me to stop bein' stupid not too long ago. Don't you think you should do the same and go after the first guy you've actually shown interest in since college? Cooper isn't just some guy."

She's right. This is totally different. This isn't just some guy... He could be so much more.

A knock at the door stops me from answering. One of the roadies opens the door with a big bouquet of roses. "Emily Young?"

"That's me." I smile. "Are those for me?"

"Sure are."

"Oh, Grace! I just got two dozen roses!" I take the card from the holder and grin.

"Cooper?" she asks with excitement.

I read the card: *A flower for every kiss I plan to share with you.*

"I think so. Whoever it was didn't sign the card." I clutch the words to my chest and grin. It has to be from him.

"Well, he's very romantic and a good guy," Grace replies. Trent's voice echoes in the back. "Em, the baby woke up, and Trent doesn't have boobs."

I laugh. "Okay, kiss Hannah for me."

"I will. Love you! Call him!"

# Chapter Five

Cooper

"Well, well, well, Wade Rycroft as I live and breathe." I clap his shoulder, and he stands.

Wade grips my hand and shakes. "Cooper Townsend. I heard you were in town."

"Yeah, just a few days. I was hopin' to run into you. I'm here for the new expo. How are you, man? How's your family?"

Our families have known each other for a long time, and our fathers are good friends. They were both young ranchers who met at an auction and stayed in touch. Wade and I bonded over the years in the rodeo circuit. He was better than I was. I'll never tell him that, though.

I grab the seat next to him at the small bar I found by the hotel. Today was draining, and I had to fight myself not to drive to Houston to see Emily. So, instead of staring at the white walls in my room, I opted for a drink.

"You know my brothers, they're the same. Rowdy as fuck and always in trouble."

"Yeah." I laugh. "As much as I wish I had brothers to help run the ranch, I'm glad it was just Presley most of the time."

"Family."

"Exactly. You still in the Army? I didn't know you were back in town."

Wade drains the beer in front of him and shakes his head. "Nope. I'm out."

"Well, thank you for your service."

He lets out a short laugh and motions to the bartender for another beer. She returns quickly with another round for both of us.

"How's the ranch?"

"I'm actually working for a security company, McKay-Taggart. Best around. Since I'm chock full of useless knowledge that doesn't apply to bein' a rancher. Army didn't prepare you for what happens when they kick you out for injuries. Nice, huh?"

There's an edge to what he says, and I realize just how much he's changed. The Wade I knew was funny and full of life. The man on that barstool is battling something deep. I was there not all that long ago. I didn't want my farm. I wanted to do anything else. I always wished I could've joined the service, but Pop needed me to take over. With my sister off in Philadelphia, it fell on me.

Being saddled with burdens I never meant to carry changed me. Left a bitter taste that made it hard to swallow. I see the same thing in Wade.

"Well, I'll buy you another beer, and you can tell me all about it."

Wade and I sit and catch up. He tells me about the McKay-Taggart security company he works for, how he isn't married, and how different it is with both parents gone. Dad attended Mr. Rycroft's funeral, said it was horrible watching all those boys look to Wade.

"Is the ranch workin' without you being there?" I ask him.

"My brothers have it handled."

He tells me more about his time in the service and the missions he went on. And, although I can't really imagine what it was like or what injuries he sustained that brought him back here, I admire what he's done.

"The company you work for now?" I press.

"Good men, most former military, which helps when it comes to this shit. You want to know whoever has your six knows what they're doing," Wade explains.

"I can understand that."

Wade nods. "I can't complain too much. I'm making good money and I'm never bored."

There's no mistaking that he's capable, it's in the way he watches everything happening in the room. I haven't glanced at the door once, but his eyes shift each time.

"You on a job now?" I ask.

"No. I just finished one and am waiting for my next assignment."

I'd be lying if I said a part of me wasn't jealous. Living a life where there's a little danger and mystery would be far more interesting than my own life. Cows are cows.

My phone vibrates in my pocket, and Emily's sweet smile fills my screen. Her long blonde hair is pulled over her shoulder and her bright blue eyes make my heart squeeze. "I need to take this," I explain to Wade and answer the call, moving toward the back of the bar.

"Hey," I answer.

"Hey, yourself."

"You finish your show?" I ask, wondering how long it would take me to drive to Houston. It's insane, but now that I've had a taste of her, I want it all.

Emily sighs. "I did."

I wish I could've seen her perform. She is truly made to be up there. You can't take your eyes off her when she's on stage. I don't think I understood what she meant when she said that music was inside her until I saw it myself.

Emily Young comes alive when she sings.

And two days ago when I watched her show, even if she wasn't singing to me, it felt like it. I know she was on that one song, but it was more than that. She made every man in that room feel like they were on the brink of something. I could feel it around me, building inside me, and at that moment, I would've done anything for her.

"You sound sad," I say as she lets out another low sigh.

"I am. I miss you, Cooper." Her voice is filled with uncertainty and fear. I want to take that away from her, and I'd be lying if I said knowing that she's even a little torn up about me doesn't make me happy.

At least I'm not the only one struggling.

I groan. "Fuck, Em. How am I supposed to wait to see you again?"

She giggles. "You could be here in just four hours."

"And then what?"

"Come and find out."

This is what has always drawn me to Emily Young. She's bold, sexy, and not afraid to say what's on her mind. She isn't like the other girls I've known. Everything about her is alluring, and I want to uncover every layer she has. The only issue is that she'll never fit into the life I have. Emily won't ever be content settled down in Bell Buckle. She's meant for the spotlight, and I'm not.

That doesn't stop me from wanting whatever I can get, though.

"Don't tempt me."

Emily's voice is warm and soft. "I wouldn't want you to miss the reason for your trip."

I don't give a fuck about my trip.

I don't even remember why the hell I'm here.

She's what has taken up every ounce of my headspace. It's as if I've glimpsed at Heaven, and it's all I can see anymore. I need to go back, taste more, see everything, have it all because I don't know if I can survive without it—even if it's only once.

I say the only thing that makes sense. "We've waited a long time for this, Emily. I think we owe it to ourselves, don't you?"

"I'll be waitin' for you."

The phone disconnects, and I need to go.

"Hey, I need to take care of something," I try to explain to Wade.

He smiles. "Sure you do."

"You know how it is." It's the way it's always been and how it always will be. "Listen, I'm only in town for a few days, but I'd love to catch up."

Wade writes his number down, and I shake his hand. "I'm around this week, but if I get a job, I may be gone without warning."

"I get it. It was good to see you."

"Good to see you, too, Coop."

We part ways, and I find myself practically running to the car. Now that I know I'm going to see her, I need to get to her immediately.

During the drive, I think about all the responsibilities I'm blowing off right now. I've never been one to walk away from something that involved the ranch. My sister was able to turn her back on things, but I couldn't.

Though I'm not the only one around to run things, so it isn't such a big deal. A year ago, I knew I needed to bring on a partner. Presley was the one who caught onto how much money we were losing because of how quickly we were growing and we couldn't keep up. I needed more help so we could scale the business, buy more land, and also sleep more than two hours a night. So, I offered the job to Wyatt Hennington, who had been my foreman for eight years. It made sense to bring him on. Between the both of us, it's allowed us to expand and grow.

*Me: I'm going to be a few more days.*

*Wyatt: No worries. We have things covered.*

*Me: I'll call you when I have more info.*

*Wyatt: What has you tied up?*

I debate what to tell him. I can be honest or play it off as something work related.

*Me: A girl.*

*Wyatt: I figured. One in particular?*

*Me: Emily.*

*Wyatt: Nice! We'll talk soon.*

This is why I like having him as my partner. He gets it. Girls make us do shit we'd never consider any other time. I've been a very patient and practical guy. I don't make a fool out of myself very often; yet, here I am, driving four hours because she said she misses me.

Women.

# Chapter Six

Emily

I chew on the tip of my thumb as I pace in the tour bus. The guys are all partying in the hotel, but I wanted to be far away from everyone.

Then I got the flowers, and all I could think about was him. How perfect he is. I was so overcome with emotion, I couldn't stop myself from texting him.

This could go very good or end in disaster. I'm not sure what I was thinking, other than I had to see him again. It was far beyond just want—it was need. Once I broke the dam, allowing the feelings to flood forward, I drowned in them.

I need his touch.

I need his arms.

I need him to give me air.

I hear a car door close, rush to the window, and my stomach flips at the sight of him.

*Okay. I can do this. It's Cooper, and I like him. He clearly likes me since he drove almost four hours, and this doesn't have to be anything more than tonight.*

Right. I'm a freaking liar and a fraud.

The knock on the door forces me to move.

When I see his face, my smile is instant. Cooper stands before me, looking a little tired and just as nervous as I feel. His deep green eyes bore into mine as he moves forward, climbing the steps without taking his gaze from mine.

"I'm here." Cooper's deep voice fills the space.

"You are."

He takes another step, and we're eye to eye. It feels like all the oxygen is sucked from the room. My head spins, and my legs grow weak. Cooper turns, closing the door behind him. I try to step back, give him room to come in, but he grips my hips, holding me firmly in place.

"I want to be clear," he says while pulling my body closer to his. "I don't know what we're doin' or where this is going, but I've never felt so…"

"Pulled?" I ask, trying to explain what I'm feeling too.

"Yeah." Cooper grins. "I couldn't get here fast enough. I had to touch you again."

My hand lifts to cup his cheek. The stubble pricks my palm, a soft scratch that reverberates all the way to my heart. He's doing something to me, and I don't think I'm strong enough to stop it. Years of wanting and wondering all come to this moment.

Here goes nothing.

"I'm feelin' the same thing. It was as if as soon as I allowed myself to see you as more than my friend—"

His lips crush down on mine, and I tangle my hands in his dark brown hair. He moves us back to where we laid the other night. Only tonight, we won't be just talking.

He sets me down in front of the bed. I see the hesitation in his eyes, but there's none in mine. I want him and whatever tonight brings. It might be fast, but I feel like we're about ten years late on doing this.

I lean forward, gripping his shirt, pulling it over his chest. My hands move across the taut skin, feeling the muscles flex beneath my fingertips. He's gorgeous. Absolutely freaking gorgeous. His body is even better than I dreamed of, and I did a lot of dreaming. I move slowly, trying to commit each dip and rise to memory. I move from his defined six-pack, up over his chiseled chest, and rise slowly to his broad shoulders, loving the way he feels against my palms. Cooper Townsend is going to ruin me for all men.

My eyes meet his, and he grins as if he can read my thoughts.

"Kiss me," I request.

Cooper moves instantly. His lips are against mine, and I drop my hands to his waist, hooking my fingers in the belt loop of his jeans, pulling him back on to the bed. He moves his hand down, slowly tracing the profile of my body. "Emily," he rasps in my ear. "Are you sure?"

I'm not sure of a lot of things, but I'm one hundred percent certain if we stop, I'll explode. All I can think about is this: there are no answers in life on if this will work. Nothing comes with a guarantee, but we have now. I know him. I know who he is, and he's a good man. He isn't some asshole who will use me and that's it.

I tug a little harder. "I'm sure that I want you. I'm sure that you get on a plane back to Bell Buckle in a few days and I don't know when I'll be home. More than anything, I'm sure I'll regret not bein' with you for the rest of my life if we stop. So, yes, I'm sure. I want this, Cooper."

He studies me for a second as he rubs his thumb across the skin on my belly. "I'm going to make sure you remember tonight."

I have no doubt about that.

Cooper's lips are against mine again, and he flips me on top of him. I straddle his body and lean up. He lifts my shirt off, exposing my breasts and pulling me to his mouth. My head falls back as he licks and sucks my nipple. I groan loudly as he moves to the other side and lavishes my breast. My fingers tangle in his hair, holding him in place.

It's been a long time since I've been with anyone. My body seems to be hyper aware of the loving it's been lacking. Either that or Cooper is just that good.

He flips me on my back so quickly that I squeak.

"Coop," I moan as I squirm beneath him.

His hands glide down my sides, removing my shorts, taking my panties with them. "You're absolutely perfect."

I close my eyes, relishing his compliment. I hadn't realized until just now how much I wanted his praise or just how thoroughly he's turning me inside out. Not once have I ever cared what a man thought of me. Sure, I work hard at keeping fit, but I also love wine and candy. However, knowing that Cooper likes what he sees causes a rush of heat to flood my body.

My back bows when he bends forward, kissing his way down my body. I close my eyes and try to get my rapid breathing under control, but it's useless. He doesn't waste a second. He runs his tongue against my clit, and I fist the sheet. "Cooper."

He repeats the motion, and I squirm. Then he takes my legs and throws them over his shoulders and begins to draw more pleasure from me than anyone ever has. His tongue circles and flicks the bud, making me shift and thrash beneath him.

I climb toward an orgasm, praying I can hold off because this feels incredible. I never want this to end, but I can't hold back. He sucks my clit in his mouth and slides a finger inside me, causing me to fall over the cliff. I scream and grip his head as I continue to plummet into the depths of the most intense pleasure I've ever experienced.

Cooper leans up with a shit-eating grin, and I try to catch my breath. He doesn't give me a second.

His lips are against mine, kissing me hard, forcing me to taste myself on his mouth.

I kiss him back, using my hands to push him up. If we only have tonight, I want to make sure it's something neither of us forgets. I fumble with his belt and button and then slide his pants and boxers off, freeing his impressive length.

My hand grips his cock, and I begin to pump. His green eyes lock on mine before his lids shut. "Fuck, Em."

"Get on your back," I request.

Cooper lies down, and my lips move to his ear. "I'm pretty sure you won't be the only one makin' memories."

He moves and takes my face in his hands. "You're going to fuckin' kill me." Cooper doesn't give me a second to respond. His mouth presses to mine, and he gives me a searing kiss. It's rough, desperate, and filled with the promise of what's to come.

My hand wraps around him, and he moans in my mouth. I want to hear all the sounds he'll make. I want to make sure that Cooper Townsend never forgets what we share here. I need to know that when he's gone, he'll think of me.

I break away from his mouth and make my way down his chest, looking up at him with a coy smile.

Cooper grins and shakes his head. "I hope you're ready for a long night, darlin'."

I smirk. "I hope you're up for it, cowboy."

"Oh, I'm definitely up for it."

I look down at his rock-hard erection and then back to him. "Yes, yes you are."

I kiss his stomach and run my tongue along the rim of his cock, loving the hissing sound that escapes his lips.

I do it again before taking him in my mouth.

Now it's my turn to make Cooper squirm.

I suck, lick, and bob my head as he moans and grunts. Cooper rests his hand on the top of my head and grips my hair gently. It spurs me on more. I love knowing I'm doing this to him. That I'm drawing this from his body.

"Fuck, Emily!"

He moves fast, and before I know it, I'm on my back and he's braced over me. Cooper's lips find mine, and I ache for him.

I've never been like this. Never have I had this insane deep need within my body for a man. Cooper pulls back and his eyes meet mine. I see the depths in those emerald eyes. The emotions swimming around that tell me he's feeling it, too.

"Cooper," I say as my voice cracks. "I-I've never felt like this…"

He kisses me slowly and then stares down at me. "Me, either."

"I need you."

"You'll have me."

He grabs a condom. I watch as he rolls it on, my body humming with excitement.

There's no going back, and I honestly don't ever want to. Cooper settles himself between my thighs, kissing me slowly as he slides in. I moan in his mouth and dig my fingers in his back. Cooper moves as our lips stay connected. Emotions rumble through me one by one. The last year I've dreamed of what it would be like. I had no idea it would be so much more.

He looks down at me, and our eyes lock. "You're going to ruin me," Cooper says.

Little does he know that he's going to ruin me right back.

We make love. There's no other way to say it. Cooper's eyes stay on mine as he gives himself to me and I do the same. I want him to feel everything I feel even though it's too much. How am I supposed to go on the road and not think of him? It's going to be impossible.

I don't care.

For right now, I hold on to the thick muscles of his arms as I start to build again. My mind fills with all the things that have happened in just a few days, and I wonder if I'm not completely insane. Cooper is everything I want and nothing I should have.

And the truth is that I'm falling in love with him.

If I'm honest with myself, I have been for a long time.

When the reality hits me, my eyes meet his, and I fall apart. Tears fall from my lashes as my orgasm rockets through me.

Cooper's lips are on mine, swallowing my cries of pleasure as he follows me over the edge.

# Chapter Seven

Cooper

What the hell am I doing?

I shouldn't be here.

I should be in Dallas, but I couldn't stay away from her. It was bad enough trying to keep Emily Young from my mind before, but now I'm screwed. I'll never be able to walk away in one piece.

I pull Emily into the crook of my arm and run my fingers against her skin. She shifts onto her side and looks up at me.

"Coop?" Her sweet, soft voice breaks the silence.

My eyes meet hers and I raise my brow.

"Are we crazy?"

I laugh. "Probably."

"What do we do now?" Emily questions.

I want to tell her to pack her shit and come home with me, which is ridiculous. I would never tell her to give up her career, her dreams, but it's what I want. I want to take her home and keep her with me. I want to wake up every day beside her.

She's perfect.

Instead, I tell her the only choice we have. "We make it work. We talk, and I'll find a way to you when I can."

Her eyes soften, and the sweet smile I love forms on her perfect lips. "I like that answer."

"I like you."

Her smile grows. "I like you. A lot."

"Yeah?" I ask with a hint of curiosity. "How much?"

"A lot more than I want to."

"Why is that?"

Her shoulder lifts and falls a little. "I think you're goin' to be a lot more trouble than you look."

I chuckle and tickle her side. "Trouble, huh?"

Emily's laughter fills the tiny room, and she squirms beneath me. This right here is everything I wanted. It feels like a lifetime of waiting, all leading me to this woman in my arms. I pull her close because a piece of me is worried this will evaporate like mist.

More than likely it will.

Emily is the girl I will never catch, the girl who shouldn't have to be contained in a goin'-nowhere town.

Sure, I'll get what I can here and there, but in the end, she'll see I'm a goin'-nowhere farmer while she's reaching for the stars.

Fuck, I'm a fool.

"Hey?" Emily touches my cheek. "You okay?"

I shake my head, trying to rid myself of the shit I don't want to think about. I can berate myself later, but right now, I want to be with her. I don't know how many moments we'll have together, so I'm damn sure going to make each one count.

"Just thinkin' about other ways to cause you trouble."

"Yeah?" She gives me a sultry smile.

I see the mischief dance in her blue eyes. I roll her onto her back, and as soon as I feel her heat, I want her again. When she grabs my ass, pulling me against her, I don't deny her.

"Oh, yeah, darlin', a whole lot of other ways."

\* \* \* \*

"Don't go back to Dallas," Emily whines from the bed.

I stand at the end in my jeans and look for my shirt. "I wish I could stay."

"But I don't know when we'll see each other again."

I climb back on the bed, crawling toward her. I kiss her gently, and she grips my neck, keeping me there. It isn't as if she has to try hard. I would stay for another night if I could. Hell, if she wanted me longer…

No, I won't go down that road now.

Today is for goodbye. I need to actually see the presentation that I flew to Texas for. If I don't get a move on, I'll miss it.

When I pull back, her eyes fill with emotion. At least this sucks for her as well. "Don't be sad, darlin'."

She tucks the sheet under her arms and looks away. "But I am sad, Coop. I don't want this to end."

"Who said it has to end?" I ask her as I pull her against my chest.

I hate seeing her like this, and the last thing I want is to leave today knowing she's sad. Not that I'm happy at the idea of driving away, but last night solidified how I feel and verified that there's no way this is the end.

Emily Young will be mine. I'm going to marry this girl come hell or high water.

She nestles her face against my neck. "I like this. I like bein' in your arms. I like it a lot more than I thought I would. A lot more than just spending a few nights together would mean with anyone else."

I push her back so I can look in her eyes. "We may have spent a few days together like this, but we've spent a lifetime building more. You're not just some random hookup, Emily. You and I have history and we're not kids."

"I know, and this is a long time coming."

That makes me feel marginally better. There is still so much I want to say to her, but the last thing I want to do is fall hard for a girl who will never be mine.

Been there, done that, and I don't want another fucking postcard.

"And hopefully a lot longer to come," I say with a twinge of hope.

"How did you make me like you so easily?"

I try not to laugh, but she looks so cute. "I'm just irresistible."

"Ehh." She shrugs.

"Ehh?"

"Well, you're somethin', all right."

I grip her chin between my thumb and forefinger, forcing her to look at me. "I'm more than that, and I'm tellin' you now that I'm not walkin' away from this. You're going to have a very persistent man waitin' for you, Emily Young. Very persistent."

Her hand threads through my hair, and she smiles. "I'm pretty persistent, too." Emily's lips touch mine and then her blue eyes bore into mine. "Stay for breakfast. Then I'll let you go without a fight."

I grapple with the fact that it'll take me four hours to get to Dallas and, if I stay, there is a very real chance I'll miss the presentation. I still have to shower, pack my things, and eventually get on a plane, but the idea of even just another hour with her ties me up. Saying no to her isn't something I want to do. Ever.

Jesus, I'm screwed.

"Breakfast, but then I *need* to go."

Emily throws her arms around my neck, pulling me on top of her. She squeals and kisses my cheek repeatedly.

This right here is why I may just sell my farm and become her biggest groupie.

I lift myself up a little and Emily hangs on. "Get ready, darlin'. I have a feeling Wyatt isn't going to be too happy with me if I don't make it back to the farm."

She gets up, gets dressed, and I can't stop smiling. I've never been this happy before. I can't remember a time in my adult life when just making someone smile like that gave me such joy.

While she finishes getting ready, I head out to the sitting area. There's a huge bouquet of red roses on the table with her name on the card.

"The flowers are nice." I try to sound offhanded.

Someone sent her flowers, and I'd be full of shit if I said it didn't bother me.

"Oh!" she yells and peeks her head in. "I didn't thank you! I'm sorry!"

"Thank me?" I ask.

"Yeah." She giggles. "Thank you for sending me the flowers, Coop. I love roses."

I hesitate, watching her. "I didn't send you flowers, Em."

She steps out of the room, and her smile fades a little. "Yes, you did. It's why I called you last night."

My brow furrows as I wonder what the hell is going on, and then I look at the card; anger mixes with jealousy as they spike through my bloodstream.

I put the card in the air and shake my head. "Is there someone else you're hookin' up with?"

"What?" She rears back.

"I didn't send these, Em." I watch as all the color drains from Emily's face.

Her lips part, and she looks terrified. "Oh, God."

I try to stay calm. She and I are extremely new, and I have no idea if there was a man before me. I clench my jaw before letting out a heavy sigh. "Is there someone else?"

Emily steps close and puts her hands on my chest. "No."

"Because I swear to God, I won't be in some fucking love triangle again."

My feelings toward Emily are so much stronger than I ever had for Grace, and I know I wouldn't survive her choosing another man over me. There's no way I'm willing to put up with that again. If she wants me, she has to choose me. I plan to show her why there is no other option.

Her hand rests on my heart, and she tilts her face so she can look at me. "There's no one else, Coop. Not even close. I'm not that girl. I genuinely thought you sent me the roses."

"I wish I had," I admit as all the anger dissipates from my body, leaving a trail of something else. Who did send her flowers about kissing her? "I should've sent you flowers."

She smiles softly. "I like having you much more than some silly flowers."

"Well, if they weren't from me, who the hell are they from?"

I don't like the idea of someone else giving her things or sending notes like this to her. I want to be the one to give her the world.

"I have no idea. Maybe it was for someone else on the tour?"

"No clue, darlin'." I look down at my watch and groan internally. "Let's talk about this later, we're runnin' on borrowed time."

"Okay, baby."

My arms tighten, and I squeeze her against me, where she fits perfectly.

# Chapter Eight

Emily

I lied.

I should've told him my suspicions about the flowers being from whoever keeps sending the letters, but I couldn't. Last thing I need is a lecture on security or to have a man overreact. Until I know what is going on, I've got it handled. I'd be full of shit if I said I wasn't concerned. This is the third thing in just a few days from this person.

However, Cooper doesn't need to be mixed up in this.

I extricate myself from Cooper's arms—begrudgingly. I hate that he's leaving, but I can't be too mad since I'll be back on the road tonight after the concert.

"Let's go before I tie you up in my room and never let you leave," I say, only half-joking.

Cooper laughs and takes my hand. We fit together perfectly in so many ways. Last night was everything and more. I fell hard, and I'm not sure I'll be able to get back up.

"I may like that," Cooper jokes.

"Oh, I know you would. I'd be very good to you."

He laughs as I pull him forward, giving me one of those playful grins. "You're killin' me."

"But what a way to go," I say over my shoulder.

We exit the bus, and there's a small line of fans standing over to the side. It's crazy how early they come just for a glimpse of Luke. Hours they stand outside in the rain and heat for autographs, but it's the coolest thing ever. One day, I pray I'll have devoted fans like that.

"Emily!" A deep voice booms from the gate. "Emily!"

I smile and wave to my one fan; I swear I've seen him before.

Cooper wraps his arm around my middle. "You have a fan."

"I do," I smile, looking up at him with my fingers resting on his chest.

His green eyes stare down at me. "A man."

I shake my head. "I know. You're observant this morning."

Cooper's lips find mine, and he holds me tight. "I'm feeling a lot of things this morning."

"Yeah?"

"Yeah, and protective is clearly at the top."

Cooper's eyes turn serious as his honesty pours through each syllable. "I'll do whatever I can to keep you safe. It's what a man should do, and more than that, it's what I'll always do."

*That is exactly why I'm hiding things from you, Coop.*

We walk, and I keep quiet, trying to wrestle with the conflicting emotions I'm struggling with. I like that Cooper feels protective of me, which is very unlike me.

Cooper, though, he is that kind of guy. The one who wants to be the rock in the relationship. You can feel it all around him. He emanates dominance, but not in that do-as-I-say kind of way, it's more of the I'm-here-and-no-one-will-hurt-you kind of way, but I also don't trust men to stay that way. I watched it with my father too many times.

"You're quiet," Cooper notes as we get to his truck.

"I know. I just want you to know there will be more male fans, Coop."

He nods. "I know. Doesn't mean I like it."

"And what about the girls who dream of the sexy and eligible Cooper Townsend?" I raise a brow while leaning against the truck.

Cooper and the Hennington brothers were every girl's dream in that town. He has no idea just how many dreams he's starred in. Which may just be a very good thing.

"Like who?" he scoffs.

I lean forward and grin. "Felicia?"

Cooper's face says it all. "Hell no. That girl is a bloodsucking viper."

"Hmm." I pretend to think. "Oh, Betsy."

His hips press against my torso, pinning me to the car. "Now that isn't even funny."

The giggle that comes from my lips is light. It's actually very funny because Betsy's mother has been trying to set the two of them up forever. It's a running joke between Grace, Presley, and me. Poor Cooper went on a blind date, only to find out Betsy's family had finally tricked him. Oh, to have been a fly on the wall.

"I'll make it up to you." I grin as I trail my finger down his chest.

"Damn right you will."

\* \* \* \*

"Do you promise to call?" I ask, vying for one more minute with him even though we've been saying goodbye for ten minutes. Breakfast was great, and now he has to leave, which is tearing me up inside.

"I don't think you could stop me."

"Good."

"Now go on inside, and I'll see you soon."

Goodbyes suck.

I've kept him here long enough. It's time to make this a little easier for him. "Okay. I'll call you after my show."

We kiss again, and he moves back, allowing me to go inside. I have a show in a few hours and could use a nap. I inhale and open the door. My heart feels as if it's being ripped from my chest as I take a step up and look back at him.

Cooper's eyes are filled with sadness, but he manages a small smile.

"Bye, Coop."

"Bye, darlin'."

I smile and close the door.

My hand rests on the door, and I fight back the rush of despair that threatens to overtake me. I need to take a nap and get my shit together. I'm living a dream that people would kill for. I have to have faith that Cooper and I will figure our relationship out.

I climb the rest of the steps and stop.

My bus is trashed.

Things are strewn around the room. Papers and my clothes are everywhere. The roses are on the floor, smashed amongst the shards from the broken vase. I move forward, assessing the damage, and there's another note taped to the window, cut-out magazine letters glued haphazardly into a single sentence: *You're playing a dangerous game.*

My heart races as I dart off the bus. Someone was on my bus. Someone went through my clothes.

I'm going to be sick. Bile climbs my throat as I struggle to catch my breath. What the hell am I going to do?

With my back against the bus, I squeeze my eyes closed and try to focus on breathing. I need to calm down, but I can't get the image of that note out of my head.

A hand touches my shoulder, and I scream. "No!"

"Em!" Cooper's voice is full of concern. "What's wrong?"

There's no stopping the emotions that explode from me. I burst out in tears and fling myself in his arms.

He holds me and tries to soothe me as I quiver and cry. It's no use, though. I'm too terrified to even get an explanation out. The notes and flowers were one thing, but that person getting on my bus is a whole other level of scary.

"Hey, talk to me," he encourages.

I swallow and know there's no way I can keep this from him anymore. "I've been getting letters and then—"

"Letters?" Cooper stiffens.

"M-my bus—" I start but then gesture to the closed door, unable to actually say it.

Cooper's eyes meet mine, and I see the shift happen. He releases me but takes my hand in his.

"I'm not letting go of you. I just need to see what happened."

Numbly, I nod, but I look at my feet, not wanting him to see my worry.

Cooper lifts my chin and waits until I look at him to speak. "I won't let anything happen to you, Emily. Trust me."

I nod again.

Holding on to him, I let him lead me back into the bus. His fingers tighten when he takes in the scene. "What the fuck?" Cooper's eyes are wide and anger vibrates off him. "How the hell did anyone get on your bus? How long have you been getting these letters, Emily?"

"I…it was…I don't k-know. It just started." I believed it was trivial, but it clearly wasn't. What if he had been in the bus when I got here? What if he had a weapon? So many things could've happened, and I thought it was just a stupid prank.

"Show me the other letters," he says through gritted teeth.

I walk back to the bedroom area, careful not to touch anything, and tears fall when I see my drawers open. My clothing is all over the bed, and I struggle to keep upright. I feel violated, and I want to go home.

Cooper's arms wrap around me, and he holds me as I lose it. My tears soak his shirt as I clutch him tight. I was so stupid thinking it was nothing. This...is not nothing. This is crazy.

"It'll be okay, baby," Cooper reassures me as he rubs my back. "Don't cry. You're going to be okay."

I look up through my wet lashes and see the promise in his eyes. "I'm scared."

"I know."

"I was so stupid," I admit.

Cooper shakes his head and sighs. "Did you think this was going to happen?"

"No."

I didn't think this was real. My dumb ass thought it was maybe some new girl joke or just part of the gig.

"The letters, darlin'," Cooper reminds me.

I walk over to the stack of letters, which is one of the only things not thrown around, and hand them to him.

He reads them each several times, not saying a word. I'm not sure what to do, but being on this bus is the last place I want to be. Who does this? Who thinks it's okay to terrorize someone's home? Even though this isn't my home per se, it's where I've been living. And where the hell was our security team when this was going on? No one should've been able to get to my bus. Luke doesn't allow anyone near the tour buses.

Eventually, Cooper puts the letters on the bed and runs his hand down his face. "This is disturbing, Em. When were you plannin' on telling me 'bout this?"

"I wasn't. I didn't think it was a big deal. Who the hell would come after me? I'm just some C-list country music singer."

He takes my hand in his. "You're not some C-list singer. You're gorgeous, talented, and clearly makin' a name for yourself. If this asshole was able to get these to you and then get on your bus, what the hell else can he do?"

A shiver runs down my spine. Now that it's clearly some whacko, there are things I need to do. "I'm going to let security know, and I know Luke won't be okay with this."

"Luke?" Cooper scoffs. "No."

"No?"

Cooper shakes his head. "No, Luke has done a shit job so far. How the hell did anyone get on your bus in the first place? How did this piece of shit go unnoticed when you are supposed to have security? He isn't going to be in charge of your safety. I will."

Here we go. I knew that Cooper would make this his fight.

"I'm not helpless. I know now that this isn't a joke. I can take care of this myself. I refused security because I can't afford it. Yes, the tour has security, but I don't. You can't come here and demand things."

He releases my hand and groans. "Have you ever taken a self-defense class? Do you own pepper spray? Are you carryin' a gun that I don't know about? Unless all of those things are a yes, then this conversation is moot."

The hell it is. I get that I may not have any of those things, but I'm not weak. There are, however, things that can be done—things that *should* be done—like telling Luke. Cooper is clearly upset, which is understandable, but I've been doing just fine on my own for thirty-eight years. I can handle this.

"I don't want to fight, but you have to understand none of this would've happened if I thought this was serious from the beginning."

Cooper cups my cheeks, and the look in his eyes stuns me. There's a mix of fear, confliction, and defiance swimming in his gorgeous gaze. "Let me do this," he requests softly. "I can't get on that plane if I think you're in danger."

My chest tightens at the tone of his plea. Am I being silly by not letting him do something to ease his fears? I look around at the devastation left by the intruder and realize how freaked out I'd be if the roles were reversed. Cooper and I may be a new thing, but there's no denying how much I care for him. If he feels an ounce of what I am, then I should give a little.

I grip his wrist and sigh. "What do you have in mind?"

# Chapter Nine

Cooper

Emily is passed out on the bed in the hotel room I got. There was no way she was staying on that bus. Fuck that. I've never seen anything like the scene there, and no matter what she thought, I was going to have someone guarding her.

My phone pings with a text.

*Wade: I'm here.*

*Me: I'll be right out.*

I check on Emily before heading out the door with the letters and photos of the bus. I believe that everything happens for a reason, and there's a damn good one that I ran into Wade Rycroft last night.

As soon as Emily agreed, I called him.

"Hey," I say, gripping his hand. "Thanks for doing this."

"I'm glad I was between jobs. Tell me more about what happened."

Wade and I talk for a few minutes as I fill him in on the letters and the bus. He looks over everything and shakes his head. "Has she had anything like this before?"

"Not that I know of." I grip the back of my neck. "It was like a fucking horror movie in that bus. The letters were one thing but then he sent her roses, too. I'm not sure if he saw the two of us together and that made him escalate this quickly."

He shakes his head as he studies the last letter. "He's clearly watchin' her. Has she said she noticed anything else? Anyone following her around? Anything out of the ordinary?"

I tell him about the guy that called out when we were walking to our car that morning. I can't remember what he looked like or even if I bothered to glance his way.

"I want to pack her shit and take her back with me," I admit.

Wade smirks. "You like her that much, huh?"

"I left the bar and drove four hours to see her. I'd say I'm pretty fucked."

He laughs. "I'd agree."

"You'll protect her?" I ask tersely. Wade is the only person I trust right now with this.

"With my life," he promises.

That's all I need to hear. I'll pay whatever to keep her safe. Emily has become more to me than I ever thought possible. As much as I want to stay here and be the one to do it, I have to get back. Presley and Wyatt know most of the business, but I can't spend a few weeks touring with her.

"I fucking hate that I have to go," I grit out.

Wade claps me on the shoulder. "I won't let anyone hurt her. This is what I'm trained for, and if I wasn't good at my job, I'd never be with the McKay-Taggart team. I know that doesn't mean much to you, but it means something down here."

It doesn't have to mean anything to me. Their reputation speaks for them. After talking to Ian Taggart on the phone, I knew there was no doubt this was the right choice and they were the only ones I could trust with her.

"If I had a doubt, she'd be hauled over my shoulder on a plane to Bell Buckle."

He nods. "I want to go look at the bus without her there. Sometimes there are details that you might not see."

"You're already on the list as the security team."

"Good. I'll be back after I check things out," Wade tells me.

We go over a few more details and then he leaves.

I make my way back up to the room and climb in the bed, wrapping my arms around her. She releases a deep breath and nestles herself against my body. Holding her like this is everything I could ever want. I don't know how I went this long denying the feelings I have for her.

Unable to stop myself, I let my fingers move against her soft skin. Her blonde hair is spilled around her head, framing her perfect face. I slide my fingers through it and move it over her shoulder. There's nothing about her that doesn't call to me. Her blue eyes are closed, but I can replicate them in my head. The denim color with tiny flecks of green that deepen when she's aroused. I rub my thumb against her plump lips, and she sighs.

I lean forward, needing to kiss her.

"Cooper," she breathes against my lips as she pulls herself out of sleep. Her hand grips the back of my neck, urging me to slide on top of her.

I kiss her hard. The emotions of the last few hours hit me, and the fear of losing her takes over. If I had left just a minute earlier, I would've never seen her rush off the bus. What if he was there watching her, too? My heart races as I kiss her with everything. Her lips mold to mine, and I touch her everywhere, needing to feel her skin.

There is no way I'd ever forgive myself if something had happened. Anger was all I allowed myself to focus on before, but the fear has wrapped around my heart, squeezing it until I'm ready to burst.

"I can't fucking lose you," I admit and then dive back into the kiss. There's no tenderness. It's pure need to feel her.

"I'm not going anywhere."

She meets my roughness, pulling me harder to her mouth. Emily's other hand claws at my back. I push up and remove my shirt, and she follows my lead and undresses. I need her. I don't care how, but I need to be inside her.

"Damn right you aren't," I agree. She's mine.

"Take me, Cooper."

That's exactly what I plan to do. "I'm not going to be sweet, baby." I let her know as I rip her shorts down. "I need to fuck you."

Emily's hands go to my jeans, yanking at the button. Her small fingers work fast, freeing my cock from my pants. "Let me ride you," she says, trying to push me on my back.

There's no mistaking the fear in her gaze. She needs this as much as I do. Both of us are searching for something to control. My instinct to give her what she's asking for overrides my own need.

I lie back, and she doesn't hesitate. Emily's thighs straddle me, and she grips my cock. Her hand pumps up and down and then she rubs herself along my shaft. Fucking hell. "Don't tease me," I warn.

Her one hand rests on my chest as she repeats the motion. I buck my hips up, needing to feel her heat. Finally, she relents and gives me exactly what we both want. She sinks down, taking me into her body as her head falls back.

My fingers grip her hips, and I set the pace. She rocks up and down, letting out noises as I lift to meet her thrusts. I watch her perfect tits bounce, revel in the sounds and smells that fill the room, inciting the pace and intensity of this moment.

"Yes!" she yells when I lean up, taking her nipple in my mouth. I dig into her back, holding her so I can suck hard. "Yes, more," she begs. My teeth clamp down, and she loses it. Emily pushes herself faster and harder than before.

"You like that, darlin'?" I ask.

"God, yes."

I'll never forget the way she looks right now. Her head thrown back, riding my cock. The look of pure pleasure on her face. "Fuck me, Emily. I want you to remember who has you right now."

She looks down, her blue eyes blazing. "I know exactly who has me."

That's it. I move quickly, flipping her on her back and plunging in before she has time to realize what happened. I pull out and then glide in slowly. I do this again, and she whimpers. Her fingers grip my ass as she lifts herself to make me go faster.

"Do you know who has you now?"

"Yes."

"Say it," I demand.

"Cooper." She says my name as a prayer.

I reward her by pushing all the way to the hilt. "No one will hurt you."

Her eyes meet mine, and she nods. "I know."

"No one else will touch you," I promise.

Emily's fingers press against my cheek. "Just you."

"I won't ever let anything happen to you," I vow.

"I trust you."

Our pace has slowed, and the anger and fear are gone. I want this to last forever. I stop completely and take her face in my hands. Everything in my life shifts right here. The way she looks at me rocks me to my core. Before I can stop myself, I say the words that are screaming in my head. "I love you."

Her lips part and tears fill her blue eyes.

Fuck. I should've kept my mouth shut.

"I thought it was just me," she says as her eyes swim with emotion. "I thought that it was too soon and that I was crazy."

My thumb wipes the tear that falls. "No, darlin'. You aren't crazy, and it's definitely not just you."

"I love you, Cooper Townsend." Her lips turn into a smile, and for the first time, I feel whole.

# Chapter Ten

Emily

"The rules are that I go where you go at all times. You don't move unless I'm with you, understand?" Wade repeats himself for the third time as we stand at the door of the bus.

"I'm not slow," I remind him. "I get it. You're my shadow, and I need to always be sure I see your silhouette."

Lame.

This is all so lame. A bodyguard...and not just any bodyguard. No, he had to get me one that's a mix of the Hulk and Thor. Wade is six-foot-two and I'm a dwarf when I'm next to him. His brown eyes narrow as I repeat after him.

"Nowhere."

I raise my hand in the Girl Scout salute. "I promise."

He grumbles and crosses his arms over his chest.

Wade is unlike the other security guys around the tour. He's dark, broody, and he exudes masculinity. Basically, he's scary as fuck. We have bodyguards on staff. I don't know why I have to have a designated one. Luke was more than capable of giving me one of his guys. After telling him about the incident, he promised his team would be on it, but Cooper wasn't having it.

Hence why Wade is here now.

"So," I say, rocking back on my heels.

"So?"

"Cooper says you guys have known each other a long time?"

"Yup," he replies while scanning the area.

"You both did rodeo?"

"Yup."

Okay. Wade only gives one-word answers, got it. Cooper is on the flight now, and I long to talk to him. My show is in twenty minutes, and I should be backstage, smiling and drinking a beer with the crew. Instead, I'm worrying about the crazy person sending me letters and trashing my bus.

"Am I bothering you?" I ask.

"Nope." Wade drops his sunglasses over his eyes, and I bite my lip. Looks like he's done with our conversation.

Cooper couldn't have found a friend who looks like he actually wants to be here?

I send him a text.

*Me: I wish you were here.*

"Emily!" Vince comes over with his arms up in the air. "Let's go, girl!"

I glance over at my new best friend, who nods.

*Here we go.*

The music blares, alerting the crowd that the show is about to begin. I stand at the edge, and my legs feel like Jell-O. I can't move. What if the guy is out there? What if he's a part of the stage crew and he's planning to drop lights on me *Phantom of the Opera* style? Maybe the guy is just going to bum-rush the stage and run away with me.

My eyes meet Wade's dark glasses, and I try to breathe.

"Are you okay?" His deep voice is low.

"No. I can't go out there. You can't go out there, and I—" My heart pounds in my chest.

Wade pulls his glasses off and steps closer. "I will always be in your line of sight."

"But what if I'm in *his* line of sight?"

"That isn't what you should worry about," Wade tries to reassure me. "All you should worry about is doing your job. I'll worry about the rest."

That sounds easy enough, only it's completely irrational to think I'm not going to be scared. There's no way I can do this. I just can't. I want to go home to Bell Buckle where no one gives a shit who I am.

Where Cooper is.

Where it's safe.

Wade's hand grips my shoulder and tears pool in my eyes. "Nothing will happen to you, Emily."

"You can't guarantee that," I counter.

His lip turns into a cocky smile. "I can."

I shrug out of his grip and look out at the microphone standing alone in the middle of the stage. That's my home, and I'm afraid to go there.

"You have a choice." Wade's voice breaks me from my stare. "You can choose to let this person win and take away your life or you can go out there and live the life you've fought for. Do you think Cooper would've left if he didn't think you were safe? If he didn't think I was the absolute best at my job, would I be here? You don't put the woman you love's safety in the hands of a novice."

Cooper's name causes my heart to race. If he didn't believe in Wade, he would be here right now. I know that without a doubt.

"I'm just scared." My voice is small and trembles at the end.

"Are you ready to get this party started?" the MC calls over the speaker.

I could throw up right now. My head starts to swim, and I know my face has gone bloodless.

"Look at me," Wade commands. "When you're out there, if you feel uncomfortable or someone makes you scared, look at me and scratch your nose. I'll grab your ass and have you off that stage before you can sing another note. Okay?"

I nod. "Okay."

The intro music cues, and I know I can't hide anymore. "Please welcome Emily Young!"

There is a time to be scared and hide and a time to step up and be brave. I have to dig deep and find the inner strength to go out there and not let fear hold me back. I've done the work, I deserve this, and I have to trust Cooper's judgment in Wade.

I plaster a smile on my face, grab my guitar, and step out into the lights.

When I stand in front of the microphone, I pretend it's like my last concert. I envision Cooper standing in the crowd. My memory recalls his smile, his eyes, and the way he makes me feel.

"Are you ready for some country music, Houston?" I ask the crowd and lose myself in the screams.

For just a second, my eyes move over to where Wade stands, and he tilts his chin in approval.

I've got this.

\* \* \* \*

"I miss you." I twist my hair while lying on my bed talking to Cooper. "I think you should just come finish out the tour with me."

"Who would make sure Wyatt doesn't burn the farm down?"

"That is true. I'm pretty sure Angie could handle him," I offer as another option. "Although, she ain't exactly a farmer."

Cooper sighs. "I wish I could, darlin'. I'd be there right now if things weren't so crazy here."

I understand, I just hate it. Every part of me wants him here with me.

"I know."

"How did the show go?" He changes the subject.

"Good. I was nervous, but I made it through."

I fill him in on some of my worries, being careful not to make him nervous as well. As much as I may say I wish Cooper were with me, I know he's where he has to be. He's invested a lot of money into Townsend Ranch. He bought his father out and then had Wyatt come in as a partner, but Cooper is majority shareholder. The two of them have really started making a name for themselves, and they even bought some land off the Henningtons to expand. It's becoming more and more of a family-owned business with them combining resources.

"You should get to bed," Cooper says through a yawn.

"Me?" I giggle. "You're probably fallin' asleep on me."

"I'm beat."

I roll over, wishing I could snuggle up next to him. "I love you, Cooper."

"I love you, too."

"I keep thinkin' all this is a dream."

He laughs. "If it is, I'd like to keep sleepin'."

"Thank you for making sure I was safe before you left. I haven't had anyone take care of me in a long time. Hell…maybe never."

My life growing up didn't have baked goods or men making sure I was set. I was lucky if my father knew I was alive. Cooper is the complete opposite of the type of guy I thought I'd end up falling for. I don't know why, but I really thought I'd be like my mama and marry some idiot who drank too much.

"If you let me, I'll make sure you never worry about anything. All I want is for you to be happy, Em. I've waited a long time for this. I'm not goin' to let it go."

Dear Lord, this man is freaking perfect.

"You make me very happy, Cooper Townsend. Very, very happy."

# Chapter Eleven

Cooper

"Are you listening?" Presley waves her hands in my face. "Earth to Cooper."

"I hear you. I'm just thinkin'."

My sister's grin spreads, and her eyes light up. I know what's coming. My nosy-ass sister is about to ask a million questions about whatever is going on with Emily. I've been able to keep the new generation of busy bodies away for the most part, but it was just a matter of time. Mama has done her digging, but thankfully Emily's family was never part of their clique.

"'Bout Emily?" Her eyes drop to her feet as she shrugs.

I'm not buying it. This has to be eating at her. Emily is part of my sister's group of friends, so there's no way this is just whatever for her.

"Wouldn't you like to know?"

"I would, in fact."

"Too bad." I start to walk out of the office and hear her behind me.

"Cooper!" She groans. "I'm your sister. You should talk to me about girls. I can help, since I am one and all."

I laugh while shaking my head. "You've never helped before."

"Umm. Grace?"

How the hell did she help with that? All she did was push her to Trent's arms. I'm not saying it wasn't the right thing, but it sure as fuck didn't give me what I wanted at that time.

"Considering Grace is married to your brother-in-law, I'm going to say you suck at helping."

"You didn't love Grace. You weren't meant for her, and you know it. I helped her and you both see that." Presley's hands rest on her hips. "We both know I'm right."

Damn her.

"Sure you are."

"You can just say thank you." Her suggestion is punctuated with a tiny tilt to her chin, which makes me laugh. She's just like our mom.

"Thank you for what? For drivin' me nuts?"

As kids, we fought like crazy, but she was my best friend. With both of us touring in the rodeo, we were forced together each weekend. My sister was amazing to watch, she shined when she raced. As we got older and she met Zach, our relationship became strained. Even if she doesn't see it, I'm glad we're past the bullshit. Having her and my nephews back in Bell Buckle has given my entire family a sense of peace. More than that, it gave me my sister back.

The ranch phone rings before she can say anything back.

"Townsend Ranch." She looks at me, saying, "Yes, he's here. Sure, may I ask who's callin'?" Her brow furrows as she listens, but then the confusion lifts and she grins. "Wade Rycroft? Is that you? It's Presley!"

I put my hand out for the phone, but she spins around and starts rambling. If Wade is calling, something's wrong. Digging in my pockets for my phone comes up short. Shit.

"Tell me about what you've been up to? Are you datin' anyone? What about your brothers? I heard you joined the Army? Was it cool?"

This conversation will last forever, and I need to know why he called. I go in search of my cell phone and finally find it in the kitchen. Sure enough, I have two missed calls. Both from him.

My sister continues talking, giving him exactly zero chances to cut in. He may be a former Green Beret and highly trained in all kinds of things, but Presley studied under my mother. He's screwed.

I dial his phone, and I hear her agree to whatever he says.

"Jesus Christ." Wade sighs as he comes on the line. "I swear she was interviewing me for a potential wife."

"She's bored and thinks everyone should be as happy as she is." I chuckle. However, I really don't care about Presley and his conversation. "I saw you called. Is Emily okay?"

"Of course she's okay. I told you that nothing will happen to her."

I breathe a sigh of relief. "Well, something happened if you're callin'."

"She got another bouquet of flowers."

"Fuck."

"I intercepted it and have my guys looking into it. We're checking with the shop that it came from to see if we can get a description of the sender or a name. I don't expect much since there's been no traces before, but what made me call was that the letter was more aggressive. It talked about how they'd find a way to each other. I'm going to analyze the language more and get to the bottom of it. Thought you'd still want to know," Wade explains.

This guy who's after her is getting out of hand. I can't keep sitting around here knowing someone is after her. "Does she know?"

"No. I didn't want to rattle her. Emily is safe, but you need to know that this asshole is only going to get bolder. I didn't tell her, but the more aware she is, the better."

"I know. I think we keep this from her for now. No need to get her worked up until we have answers." The selfish part of me wants to tell her and have her come here. We could spend our days together and make love all night. The other half of me knows that wouldn't be what's right for her.

I know what it's like to have your choices stripped from you.

"Luke is talking about extending the tour," Wade says. "He's thinking of adding another two weeks on."

"Talkin' about it or doin' it?" I ask as I run my hand down my face.

"No idea. I only know because one of the other security guys heard it."

When we talked yesterday, she sounded like the girl I've always known. She was happy about her performance and that one of the radio hosts made an effort to talk to her. They were looking at her coming on his morning show, which is the break she's been waiting for. So, I'm not sure that telling her about this is a good idea.

I close my eyes and lean against the counter. "If something else shows up, then I'll tell her."

"It's your call, Coop." I hear the grit in his voice. "I'll let you know if anything else happens."

"Thanks."

We disconnect the call, and I grapple with my decision. Emily's safety is first and foremost, but she was freaked out last week to the point she almost couldn't go on stage. My gut says that Wade can handle it and if he was concerned, he would have told her right then.

Still, if anything happens to her, I'll never forgive myself.

* * * *

They extended the tour for two more months.

Not two weeks.

Two fucking months.

"I'm sorry, Coop." Emily's face is full of sorrow. I hate this shit. There's no way to hide the disappointment from my face.

Her blue eyes swim with tears on my screen. "Don't cry, baby. We'll figure it out."

"I just can't quit on this tour. It would be career suicide," she says, tucking her hair behind her ear.

She's so beautiful. All I want right now is to touch her, taste her, love her, but I have to wait.

The farm experienced a huge blow this week. Someone cut the fence, and we lost about a third of our herd. If I didn't have to talk to another investigator today and insurance adjuster tomorrow, I would be on a plane right now.

"And I can't come to you."

She rests her cheek on her fist. "Any luck on the herd?"

"No. Trent hasn't really had a crime since he's been the sheriff so he's no help."

Emily laughs. "I'm sure he's all excited to do some real police work."

"Well, if he can call it that."

He tries his best, but I'm thinking he got his training from watching cop shows on television. Even Wyatt makes fun of his brother half the time. I know finding whoever did it is a long shot, but replacing a third of the herd is going to cost me a fortune. Hopefully, our insurance will cover most of it.

"Hold on, honey. Someone is at the door." Emily puts the phone down, and I hear a deep voice in the background. Her face fills the screen a few seconds later. "Wade wants to talk to us," she says, holding the phone so I can see both of them.

This can't be good.

It's been five days of quiet. I'd hoped...

"We had another delivery. This time it's a file with photos." He clears his throat and looks directly at Em. "I want you off this bus right now."

"What?" she asks.

Wade takes the phone from Emily. "I'll send you an email in ten minutes. I'm going to secure Emily and then I'll fill you in."

Anger, fear, and nervous energy floods me, demanding I get answers now, but I nod in agreement. Emily comes first.

"Get her safe, and I'll be waiting for your call."

# Chapter Twelve

Emily

I'm shivering. No matter how many blankets Vince and Luke wrap around me, I can't get warm. My fingers are frozen, and I can't breathe.

He had a video camera in my bedroom.

"You'll stay with us," Luke says, trying to reassure me. "We'll add more security to your team as well. Whatever you need, Emily."

I need Cooper.

Wade is on the phone with him now. Cooper's too angry to talk to me. The photos were graphic. I was naked in each one. He has photos of me after a shower from two days ago. Pictures of me talking on the phone with Cooper. Pictures that, in the wrong hands, could destroy my life.

I look at Luke with tears falling down my cheek. "Why me? Why now? I haven't done anything to anyone. I've never flirted or given the illusion I was lookin' for something. I'm just tryin' to sing."

He wraps his arms around my shoulders and rubs a hand up and down my back. "This isn't your fault."

"How does this happen, Luke? How is this person getting access to my bus?"

Vince gets to his feet and starts to pace. "It's someone on the crew."

Luke nods. "It's the only thing that makes sense."

I curl my legs tighter to my chest and rest my forehead on my knees. There are so many guys on the crew that it could be anyone. My mind searches for anyone that stands out, but it's just a sea of faces that all blend together. For the most part, they're all quiet and don't pay me much attention. My stage setup is basically nothing.

My band uses Luke's equipment since it's too expensive to tow our own, and I don't have any fancy lights or backdrops.

"I should leave," I say, wiping another tear.

"Leave?" Luke pulls back. "You can't leave. We have two months left and you're gainin' traction on the radio. If you quit, what happens then?"

Not even an hour ago, I was telling Cooper the same thing. But that was before I saw those photos.

The door opens, and I jump. Wade's eyes meet mine, his features softening as he sees my tears. "I searched the bus. We got everything."

"I can't..."

Wade looks at Luke with the anger back in his eyes. "I'm taking her to the bus. I'll be interviewing everyone on this tour. There *will* be full cooperation from your people, right?"

Vince moves closer. Both Luke and Wade look ready to punch the other. "My people will look at the crew."

"And if the guy we're looking for is one of your people?" Wade's chest puffs out. He's much taller than Luke, and I'm pretty sure he could snap him like a twig. Luke has the good sense to consider this, but then his jaw clenches in denial and Wade digs harder. "Your team hasn't done a damn thing to protect Emily. They're supposedly prescreening her mail, yet this is the second package to make it through."

"Second?" I look up. "What do you mean the second package?"

He doesn't spare a glance at me. Wade points his finger at Luke's chest. "I'm the lead on this from now on. Your team reports to me until we find out who this fucker is, got it?"

I stand, letting the blankets fall to the floor. "What do you mean the second package?" I yell, pushing my way between them.

"Not now."

"I'll give you not now! I want to know what the hell is goin' on! Someone isn't stalking any of you. This person is after *me*. None of you get to decide what information I get or not." I glance at all three of them with frustration. How dare they keep things from me? I thought this was the first time in over two weeks.

"We'll talk about it all later," Wade says through gritted teeth, and he looks back at Luke.

I stare at him, waiting. "Now."

Wade's eyes drop to mine, and he huffs. It's clear that he's used to obedience, but I don't care. I want answers. This information should never have been kept from me. "Fine. You got flowers, but I handled it, and Cooper and I agreed it was best to wait until we had something substantial."

"Oh, you did, did you?" I spit the words at him.

Unreal.

I grab my phone and glare at Wade. "Since you and Cooper decide everythin', why don't I give him a call and he can tell me what exactly I'm allowed to know. You two are ridiculous."

"Emily," he warns, but I don't care.

Before I can press send, a loud siren type sound blares through the radio on Wade's belt. Panic splays on everyone's face except his.

Wade looks calm.

Wade looks collected.

And he looks deadly as he reaches to silence the alarm without taking his eyes from me.

"What's happening?" I ask.

"Stay here." Wade grips my shoulders. "I mean it, don't leave this trailer. I'll be back."

"I'll stay with her," Luke says.

He doesn't look happy, but he's already moving toward the door. "Don't let her out of your sight," Wade demands and then he's gone.

I stand here with Luke, feeling sick to my stomach. The images in the photos fill my mind.

Me standing there, looking at my phone with a smile on my lips as I get dressed.

Just getting out of the shower, completely naked, my breasts completely in view as I pull my underwear on. Every part of me was on display for his enjoyment, and now people who never should have seen me that way now have.

"I know you're upset." Luke's Southern twang breaks me from my thoughts.

"That's an understatement."

"Look, I promise you this is going to be handled."

Keeping my eyes down, I release a heavy sigh. If only it were that easy. No one can put this genie back in the bottle. The truth is, I'm scared, angry, hurt, embarrassed, and so much more. All I wanted was to have people listen to my songs, not this.

"I appreciate it."

"Luke, bring Emily to the stage! Now! Get off the fucking bus!" Someone yells as they bang on the door. I can hear people yelling to each other and fear floods my veins.

"Let's go," Luke urges.

"But," I protest. Wade said to stay here. "He said…"

He grips my arm, pulling me to my feet. "What if there's something on this bus?"

I get up willingly after he says that and let him drag me through the parking lot and closer to the stage. All the security lights are off, but just being away from the buses lets me breathe easier.

"You okay?" he asks as we climb our way to the stage.

"Not really, but what choice do I have?"

Luke nods. "I always feel better here," he says as we reach stage left.

"What's goin' on out there? Do you know what the alar—" I get cut off by a loud bang.

"What the?" Luke says as he looks to where flashlights are moving around, and I can vaguely see the gate area where the majority of everyone is.

I move, trying to get a better view. "Luke? What was that?"

I swear I'm in the middle of some horrible scary movie. Lights, people yelling at each other, and it feels like it's surrounding me.

"I don't know. Stay here. I'm going to see if I can get some answers and I'll be right back, okay? You're safe. No one knows where you are but me, and I'll tell Wade."

"Okay."

He runs off and I move to the only place I feel like I belong—center stage.

Just this evening I stood here, feeling like my life was close to perfect. My dreams were coming true and trouble was behind me. I wondered how long Cooper would demand Wade stay around since my stalker was gone.

I was so wrong.

My chest heaves from the run, and I look out at the vacant seats. Vast emptiness is all around me and inside me.

Wade should've told me.

Cooper should've told me.

Just the thought of his name brings back the images I was trying so hard to forget.

The next photo of me lying on the bed in Cooper's shirt as I smile with the phone to my ear.

Moments that were mine—stolen.

I grip the phone in my hand, needing to tell him how wrong he was for keeping things from me.

Cooper answers on the first ring. "Em," he says my name as a sigh.

"You lied to me! You kept the flowers from me, and this guy put a goddamn camera in my bedroom, Cooper! If I'd known this was still happening, I would've been vigilant. I thought it was over!" Tears of anger flood my vision as my emotions pour out. "I *trusted* you! I thought you understood that this was my problem to handle."

He releases a heavy breath. "I was protecting you. Wade was taking care of things. Why worry you?"

I swipe the tears, but more fall. "I'm not some damsel in distress. You lied to me that everything was fine and I was safe. All the while, this man was lookin' at me sleep, shower, and live."

"I know, and I hate myself right now." His voice breaks, and so does my heart.

"He...he took..." I start to fall apart. "He took *everything* from me! He saw me when I was raw and vulnerable. He invaded my privacy, Cooper!"

"I'll be there in two days, Emily. I'm on a plane as soon as I finish my meeting. I'll get back what he took from you, darlin'. No one is going to hurt you."

I sink down to the stage and try to slow my breathing. I just got done telling him that I didn't need him to save me, and as much as I want to call foul on myself and tell him to come, I know he's dealing with his own mess as well. He can't just keep dropping things to run to my side. I'm not that girl. "But the farm."

"The farm isn't my concern. You are."

I love this man. I love him so much my heart can't contain it all, but I'm so angry and confused and...lost. "I don't know..."

"There's nothing for you to know other than in forty-eight hours I'll have you in my arms and no one will get close to you."

My hand clutches the base of my neck, and I pray that isn't a lie. I want to see him more than anything. Even in my hurt, I crave him.

I see Wade standing on the side of the stage with his arms crossed over his chest. "I'll see you soon. Wade has a lot to fill me in on."

"All right, darlin'. I'll see you soon."

I stand and pull myself together, ready to face a very pissed-off big man who could crush me. Even though I didn't do anything wrong, his profile doesn't scream happy or relieved.

"Em?" Cooper calls out.

"Yeah?"

"I'm sorry you feel I betrayed you. I'll never lie to you."

Guilt wraps around my chest, squeezing tight. "I know you were only doin' what you thought was right."

"I love you." Cooper's deep rasp is laced with emotion.

"I love you, too."

Wade moves toward me as I disconnect the call, and I brace myself for whatever he has to fill me in on. God only knows what made those alarms ring or where the hell Luke went.

"Is everything okay now?" I start as I make my way toward him, knowing nothing about this is going to be good news.

"Hello, Emily." The deep voice that isn't Wade's causes my heart to plummet. "Glad I finally got you alone."

# Chapter Thirteen

Emily

"What do you want?" I take a step back as he moves closer.

"Don't walk away, sweetheart. I've been waiting a long time to have your attention all to myself." The man keeps himself in the shadows.

I pray that Luke comes back now. I grip my phone, contemplating whether I can get a call out without the man in front of me noticing.

"You and I haven't had time alone in a while." He hums with satisfaction. "I've missed you."

I can't place his voice. It's familiar, but nothing is ringing a bell.

Every muscle in my body tenses, and I glance to the neon exit sign before deciding the emergency exit just off stage is closer. "You have?" I flip the phone backward to hide the light.

His silhouette shifts to the curtain a little farther back, further shielding his face. "I did, up until the last few weeks."

My heart is pounding so hard against my chest I swear he can hear it. "What changed?" I ask and try to follow his movements, but he's staying completely out of the light.

"I think you know, baby."

His term of endearment makes me sick. "I really don't."

His chuckle is menacing. "Maybe you should call Cooper Townsend again," he suggests.

My breathing accelerates, and I struggle to hold on to control. "Cooper?"

"Don't play stupid," he warns. "I know all about your new boyfriend. I was actually just in Tennessee this week..."

I can almost hear the smile in his voice. This guy is completely insane, and I've never been more terrified of anyone or anything in my life. "Why were you there?"

"Just checking on things..." He moves again, and I take a step back.

Nothing about what he's saying makes sense. My hands start to shake, bile burns my throat, and I can feel the band of tightness restricting my lungs. I have to get a call out to someone. I push the button, and the phone brightens the dark space. He makes a low, menacing sound.

"Don't think about it," he warns. "If you try to call for help, you'll push me to do something drastic. Put the phone on the ground."

My hands hold tighter, wanting to do the opposite of what he's requesting. Now, I'm the dumb girl on television who you scream at not to listen to the attacker.

"You know, there's a lot of things in your hometown that I never knew about. Did you know there was some big crime that happened?"

I gasp and know without him telling me that he is the one who cut down Cooper's fencing. "Why are you doin' this?" I ask breathlessly.

"To show you the lengths I'll go to keep us together, baby. I'm the one you're supposed to be with," he says with conviction. "I'm fighting for you, Emily. He's worried about his precious cows, and I'm here for you. He doesn't deserve you, and I'll keep showing you his true colors. Now, drop the fucking phone."

My fingers release the lifeline I had, and I pray he doesn't hurt anyone. Most of all Cooper. "Please," I beg. "Please don't do anything to him. You don't have to do this."

The man's deep sigh filters around me. "All you have to do is see what I'm showing you. Once you get rid of him, you and I can be happy. Otherwise, you'll piss me off, and I'll have no choice..."

Tears begin to fall at his threats to hurt Cooper. "I'm sorry," I say, hoping he'll stop. "I didn't mean for this to happen."

"Stop crying!" he yells, and I stagger back. "You don't fucking cry for him in front of me."

"I wasn't." The lie comes out in a broken mess of words. It's clear that Cooper is an issue, so I change the subject to my stalker. "I'm cryin' because I was stupid not to see what you're saying is true. I was so stupid, and I'm sorry!"

He moves out from behind the curtain, but not enough for me to see anything other than he's tall, has dark hair that's cut close to the skin, and is dressed in all black. "Turn around. Face the audience," he commands. "We'll see each other once you've earned it."

I want to scream and run, but I have no idea if he's armed or if I could even outrun him. I slowly spin, trembling.

*Please, God, don't let me die.*

I stand here, without any idea if he's going to hurt me. He touches my shoulder, and I start to scream, but his hand quickly covers my mouth.

His hot breath is against my ear. "Don't scream or I'll have to teach you a lesson." I don't even try to stop the tears that burn down my cheeks. "We could be so happy." His nose moves against my neck, up into my hair. "You can make it all stop, baby. It's only because you forgot about what we had."

He pushes his body against mine, and another tear falls.

"Just give us our time back and get rid of the man who isn't good enough. Do you want me to hurt him? Is that how you want me to get rid of him? Will that be how you finally believe how much I love you, Emily? Do I need to kill him to show it?"

The blood runs cold in my veins. I will not let Cooper be hurt by this man, and I will do or say anything as long as it gets him to let me go. So I shake my head quickly. When he drops his hand, I speak. "No, I'll give us a chance."

This can't be real. This is just a nightmare. It has to be, because Wade would be here if it was real. He has to be coming here any second now.

"I knew you'd come around." He grazes his teeth against my ear. "Your little *protector* may have found my cameras, but remember that I'm always listening. I won't hesitate to remind you how much Cooper doesn't love you if you tell the dog about our little chat. I love you. I'm willing to do *anything* to have you."

He presses his lips to the side of my head, and I bite my tongue to keep from screaming out.

"I'll see you soon, my sweet little nightingale. I'm always around."

I feel the heat from his body disappear. I turn quickly, but all I see is the back of his head as he runs off the stage and out of view.

My legs go limp, and I fall to my knees. He's the reason Cooper lost his herd. He's been able to get in my bus not once but twice that I know of. There's nothing he won't do, and I know, deep down in my soul, that he'll hurt Cooper if I don't obey.

With trembling hands, I dial Wade's number.

"Where the fuck are you?" he growls through the phone. "I told you to stay on the fucking bus!"

"The stage," is all I'm able to say before I completely fall apart.

Minutes later, I hear footsteps and Wade's voice. "Emily!" He rushes over.

My eyes meet his, and even in the dark, I'm sure he can see the tears. "Please take me somewhere. I can't walk."

"Are you hurt?"

"Not physically." I go for a half-truth.

I can't tell Wade about what happened just moments ago. Not here. Not now. The psycho is clearly listening, watching, and God only knows where he is. Being quiet is all I can do. There are times I believe in trusting my gut—this is one.

"Did you fall?" Wade's hands brush over my arms and legs as if he's checking for injuries.

Oh, I fell. I fell into the hands of a stalker who wants to kill my boyfriend.

I fell in love, only to have it torn away.

I fell into the depths of hell, and the only way out is a deal with the Devil.

Instead of saying any of that, I shake my head. "I'm tired."

"You're lying." He studies me and then glances to the shadows around us. "Something has you rattled and you need to tell me what. Why did you leave the bus?"

"Luke was supposed to be right back," I say as my lip trembles.

"What the fuck?" He looks around. "I'm going to kill him."

Wade is a good man, and I wish I had trusted in that. He's been here ensuring my safety for weeks, and I failed him.

Now, it's Cooper I'm worried about.

If this guy is willing to go all the way to Bell Buckle to prove some sick point, I have no doubt he will make good on his threat if Cooper shows up here. I start to cry harder, each tear is an outward display of the pain I'm in. I don't want to do this, but I don't have a choice.

"Talk to me, Emily," Wade urges.

I look up at him, and the knot in my stomach twists. "It's over. It's all over."

"What's over?" His voice drops to a whisper. "Is he here?"

I shake my head. "No. I mean me and Cooper."

Another loud sob escapes my lips, and I cling to Wade. Everything is falling apart, and I have no hope left.

"I'm sure you'll work it out." Wade tries to comfort me, but he's not very convincing, and I cry harder. "Cooper won't let you go, not without fighting the world. I've seen what a man will do for the woman who owns him."

Too bad it isn't Cooper's choice. I'm the only one who knows his life is in danger at the hands of a psychopath. One who will stop at nothing to get me.

There's only one option.

I have to walk away from the only man I've loved to keep him safe.

"Please, just take me away from here," I beg.

Wade doesn't hesitate. He hooks his arms under my legs and pulls me to his chest. My arms wrap around his neck, and I hold on.

I'm lost inside my hopeless thoughts. My eyes are open, but I don't see anything. His words ping pong around my head, bouncing from one terrifying thought to another. I'm going to have to hurt Cooper.

I'm going to lie to him.

I need to find a way to make him stay in Bell Buckle because he won't listen if I just tell him to. He'll fight back and show up regardless.

Wade carries me back to the bus without complaint. He climbs the stairs and sits me on the couch. I immediately curl into myself.

"Emily." He touches my face, and my tears continue to drop.

Something hits me. Wade works for Cooper. I lift my head and sit up quickly. "Will you break the contract with Cooper?" I ask.

"What?"

"Will you end your contract with him and work for me?" I clarify.

Wade scratches the back of his head with his ball cap. "I'm telling you there's no way he's going to fire me."

I shake my head. "I didn't think he would. I'm asking you to work for me. I don't want Cooper involved."

He takes a seat next to me. "This is going to blow over."

"No. It isn't." I wipe my face and look away.

I can't let it.

"I know you're upset, but he is trying to protect you."

I can't talk about this. I don't know if the crazy man who wants to hurt Cooper to win me is listening. The pain of what I'm about to do slices through me. My chest aches, and I try to hold myself together.

"Can you please let me have a few minutes to myself?" I ask Wade. "I want you to stop relaying anything about me to Cooper. Can you do that?"

He sighs and drops his head. "Sure." I hear the disappointment in his voice, but it's vital they don't communicate.

"Thank you. I'll pay the fees for my protection if you need it to be black and white. I need you to ignore Cooper's calls because this is no longer his concern."

Wade's eyes meet mine. "I technically work for him."

"Do you want me to fire you?" I ask, praying he'll say no. I need Wade more than ever. Even if I'm lying to him.

"Fine. Twenty-four hours, but after that, I'll need to figure out how we're going to handle this."

He walks off the bus with frustration radiating off him.

Now to make the phone call that will officially destroy me.

# Chapter Fourteen

Cooper

When I see Emily's face flash on my screen, I answer. "Hi, darlin', are you okay?"

"No. I'm not. I thought I was okay with everything, but I'm not."

I sit up in my bed and turn the light on. She sounds angry again.

"I thought we talked about this." I'm not sure what changed in an hour. We were fine, talking about me coming there, and now she's pissed again?

Emily's breathing quickens. "I don't want you to come here. I want time alone."

What the fuck? This is completely different from what she said before. "What changed?"

"Everything."

I swear that women confuse the shit out of me. "Can you elaborate please?"

"This was just the eye opener I needed. This can't work between us. We were fooling ourselves, and I think it'll just be easier to sever things now. A clean break."

Okay, now I'm completely fucking floored. She has never mentioned a damn word about having any doubts. We've talked every single day. Our conversations have been about how to make things work. Who could travel when and finding ways around the shit in our way. Both of us were on board. I don't know where the hell this is coming from.

"I understand you're upset, but—"

"No, it's over."

"No, it's not," I reply. "It is not over... We're going to talk about this."

She laughs. "There's nothing to talk about, Cooper. We're done. I'm done."

"Well, I'm not done." I'm not letting go of her. I love her, and I'll fight to the ends of the earth to keep her. She's the girl I've waited my whole life for. There's no way I'm going to walk away because she has a few doubts.

Fuck that.

"It's not up to you!" Emily yells. "I don't want to do this with you anymore. I don't love you. I was foolin' myself."

"Bullshit!" This is insanity. She's lying to me, and I know it. I saw the way she looked at me. I hear it in her voice when we talk. "If you're scared, I get it, but I'm getting on that plane in two days. You're not goin' to end this on the goddamn phone. If you want to end this, you need to say it to my face. I want to see you look me in the eyes and tell me you don't love me."

Her breath hitches. "Do you really want to see this, Cooper? Is that what you want? You want me to hurt you?"

My heart pounds against my ribs and two words stick out. "See what?"

"Look." Emily sighs. "I...I didn't want to... It just happened..."

"Just say it," I say through gritted teeth.

If this is what I think it is, I'm going to lose my mind. I get to my feet and start to pace because deep in my gut I feel it. This is going to fucking kill me.

After a few seconds of silence, she clears her throat. "I have feelings for someone else."

Rage consumes me. Every part of me wants to explode and release the fury that builds inside. "Are you fucking kidding me?"

My breathing is heavy, and I grip the edge of the door.

"It just happened. It's been buildin' for a while, and tonight, it finally came to a head."

"Just happened?" I let out a sarcastic laugh.

"Cooper..." Emily's voice is barely a whisper. "Please, I didn't want to hurt you. I really didn't. I'm so sorry!"

That's just fucking perfect. I really don't give a shit if she's sorry.

An hour ago, she told me she loved me. Three hours ago, we were videoing about how much we wanted to be together. All of it was a lie. This whole time, I've been worried sick about her and she's going behind my back?

"I thought you were different." I hear the defeat in my voice. "I thought you were the one. I guess I was wrong."

She lets out a heavy cry, and I'm being torn apart. I want to comfort her, but she's the one breaking me. "I swear it wasn't like that." Emily cries harder. "I wanted us to work, but it was like it wasn't my choice."

I've known this girl my whole life, and she doesn't do anything she doesn't want to do. "Who is it?" I ask, needing to know.

Emily falls quiet.

"You owe me that much!" My palm hitting the wall sends out a loud echo.

I hear her sniffle as she struggles to catch her breath. I imagine her blue eyes being red rimmed, her blonde hair falling around her face, and I tighten my fist. She was mine. I would've given her the world, and now I've lost her to someone else.

"Please," she pleads. "Please don't make me say it."

Do I want to hurt her? No. But I've been here before. I was the loser in the last relationship because Grace chose another man. Emily is supposed to be my happy ending. She is the girl who chose *me*.

"I want to know his name. Is it Luke? Is it Vince?" I taunt. "Who is the guy you're willing to throw away all we were buildin' for? Who could you have possibly met that could love you, protect you, and be there for you the way I will?"

Nothing in the world could prepare me for the next word out of her mouth. "Wade."

\* \* \* \*

"No," Grace says as she tries to convince me I misunderstood. "She loves you. I know she does."

Why I came here, I'll never know. I hung up the phone, threw it against the wall, and watched it shatter in dozens of pieces.

I grabbed my keys and drove. Somehow, I ended up at my ex's house with her husband staring at me with a grin.

Grace takes my hand in hers. "I don't know what's goin' on with her, but I know Emily, and this isn't like her. She's never been in love, Cooper. She's always kept herself so distant from men, but with you, she allowed herself to open up. I can't see her throwing that away, not for some guy she just met."

If only that were the case, but she clearly doesn't give a shit. My lifelong friend and the girl I hired him to protect. I'm at a complete loss.

"History repeating itself again," I mutter.

"You know it wasn't that way for us."

She's right. For Grace and me, it was never going to work. I knew that from day one, but I had to try. I thought maybe I could give her what she wanted that Trent wouldn't. Presley warned me early on that Grace's heart was never mine to win, but I refused to listen.

I knew it, and in retrospect, it was never her. It was Emily, but I had been too chicken to ever admit that.

Emily was the girl that I looked at but never really saw.

I'd been too scared to look. I knew if I did, she would own me, and I was right.

I get to my feet and look at the ceiling. "How the hell is this happening? How could Wade, of all people, do this to me?"

"You don't know anything at this point," Grace reminds me.

I have no phone so there's no way of getting a hold of Wade now.

Trent starts to laugh quietly. Is he for real? He's laughing at this. I swear to God, he and I may be cool, but his arrogance sometimes pisses me off.

"What the hell are you laughing at?"

The oldest Hennington brother gets to his feet and chuckles. "Karma, man."

"Trent!" Grace admonishes him.

"No." His eyes cut to mine. "It sucks when your friend moves in on the girl you love, right? You feel ten times more betrayed. You feel like every part of you is suddenly disconnected. Losing her is bad enough, but losing her to someone you trust...it's brutal, huh?"

"That was different," I defend. Grace left him before she and I had any kind of relationship.

He rolls his eyes as he gets to his feet. "You may not want to hear this, but it wasn't different for me. Whatever way you spun goin' after Grace in your head, it wasn't justifiable to me."

Grace stands, placing her hand on Trent's forearm. "That was years ago, and we've all long since buried the hatchet."

Seems someone is ready to chop wood again.

He releases a heavy sigh. "I'm not mad, I'm just clueing him in a little."

"Thanks for that." My sarcasm is thick.

"You're welcome."

Grace lets out a groan as her head falls back. "Men!"

Trent grips my shoulder and clamps down. "Listen, I'm not tryin' to drudge up old shit. I got the girl, I'm not pissed."

Once again, the urge to clock him is real. "Are you always this fucking helpful?"

"Pretty much. My question is this... Do you love her?"

With everything inside me.

"Yes."

"Would you do anything for her?"

I don't hesitate. "Yes."

Trent nods. "Including the fight of your life? Are you willin' to go to war to get your girl? Will you put all your stupid bullshit aside for her? Because that's what all this talk has been, Coop. Bullshit. You're talkin' about Wade this and that, but when I lost Grace, I went insane. I saw her slippin' away, and I manned the fuck up." He wraps his arm around Grace's waist, pulling her against his side. "I told you that night that you had no idea how I felt, and now you do. The question is... What are you goin' to do about it?"

# Chapter Fifteen

Emily

"You have to get up," Wade says while banging on my door. "It's been two days since you've gotten out of bed."

I don't care. I'll stay here until I feel like living again. Besides, when we're driving and waiting for the next show, what does it matter anyway?

My phone lies on my bed with no missed calls. No returned text messages. Nothing from Cooper.

I did exactly what I was supposed to do, and now, I'd like to stay in my little hole. Now I understand why Presley and Grace were so damn miserable. Broken hearts hurt more than broken bones.

The pain is indescribable. It's like a living thing inside my heart, turning everything cold and dark. I was smart to avoid this shit.

Another knock. "Emily, I'm letting Ginny in," Wade says.

Great, this should be epically fun.

"Emily Young, you get your skinny ass out of this bed right the hell now!" Ginny says as she throws the door open.

"Go away." I pull the covers back over my head.

"Get up!" The blanket is gone, and she's gripping my ankle, yanking me down the bed. "I did not bust my ass to get Luke to put you on this tour, just to have you throw it all away. You're going to be a goddamn professional and get your ass on that stage, so help me God."

Doesn't she see the pain I'm in? There must be a gaping hole where my heart used to be, because it's gone.

"I can't sing. I can't breathe!" I sit up and tears start to form.

"I can see that you're a mess, but no one gives a shit. You want a chance in this business?"

Right now, I really don't give a shit.

Wade leans against the door, watching this go down. "You're some bodyguard. I'm being physically assaulted and you just stand there?"

"Yeah, Ginny is really doing a number on you by making you get up and shower." He takes a bite of his apple. "That's a real threat to your safety. Plus, you're supposed to be paying my salary so you need to work. I'm doing what's in my best interest."

Smug cowboy.

He's telling the truth, though. Yesterday, he told me he's adding two additional members to the overall team. They'll be in charge of personal effects and focus on ensuring no one can access my bus especially. While I was hosting my pity party, Wade installed security cameras in my bus so we know if anyone manages to get past outside security. Then, he's talking about bringing another member from McKay-Taggart since Luke's security team is clearly a bunch of idiots. His words, not mine.

This all sounds great, but the fact is, it isn't me I'm worried about. It's Cooper.

She cups my chin and pulls it toward her. "I get that the man I told you to stay away from hurt you. I'm sorry that you're broken, but you sing country music, honey. Go out there and tell it in your music."

"I can't go on that stage," I murmur as I look away.

Standing in the same place where he threatened me and the people I love... I'm not strong enough. I glance up to find Wade watching me suspiciously.

"You're quitting then?" Ginny asks.

I could never. Music is who I am, but I can't imagine going out there.

"She'll be ready in an hour," Wade answers.

"Excuse me?" *I don't think so, buddy. You don't get to tell me what I'm doing.*

"I said you'll be ready for your show. You want me to stay on as your bodyguard, then you need to actually leave the damn bus. Otherwise, there's no reason for me to be here. You have your panic button, a security team, as well as cameras installed to keep you safe. Get up, get ready, and sing your pretty little heart out."

My jaw drops. "You work for me. I'm in charge."

He laughs and then takes another bite.

"I like him," Ginny notes. "I'll see you in an hour."

Both of them leave the room, and I flop back on the bed.

My phone dings, and I grab it quickly, hoping it's Cooper.

*Grace: What the ever-loving hell have you done?*

Disappointment strikes me that it isn't him. He must hate me.

I hate me.

*Me: Please don't...*

*Grace: You fell in love with your bodyguard? Really? Cooper is a good guy, Em.*

Like I don't know that. He's a good guy that doesn't deserve to lose his herd. He's a good guy who doesn't need some crazy asshole trying to kill him just to prove his undying love to me. It isn't what I want. None of this is.

I want Cooper.

I want our love, but sacrificing your own happiness is sometimes what love is.

I'm doing the unselfish thing by letting him go.

*Me: Don't forget that you're married to Trent and not Cooper.*

It's a low blow, but she doesn't have the right to judge me. I'm not actually dating Wade. Hell, I can barely stand his bossiness most days.

*Grace: I know how my story played out, honey. It's yours that I'm worried about.*

*Me: Tell me this gets easier. Tell me that I will stop feeling like I'm the worst person in the world.*

*Grace: Oh, Em. I wish it did.*

I bite my thumbnail, debating whether I should ask her if she's seen him. I'm assuming she heard about the breakup from Presley.

*Me: Is he okay?*

*Grace: Not really. He lost you to another man that he hired to protect you. I'm not really sure what you're thinking.*

Neither am I.

"Fifty minutes," Wade yells from the other side of the door.

Ugh. "I never said I was doing it," I reply.

"You either get your ass in the shower on your own or I'll strip you down and put you in there myself," he warns.

He wouldn't dare. Would he?

Not wanting to take any chances, I get up and lock the door, not that I think that'll actually keep him out, but hopefully it's a deterrent.

I shoot a text off to Grace before GI Joe decides it's time for a shower.

*Me: I have to get ready for my show. Can I call you later?*

*Grace: Of course. Just think about what you're doing. I hate to see you give up something we both know you've wanted for a long time.*

"Forty-five minutes," the pain-in-the-ass-guard's voice reminds me.

"Who needs alarm clocks when they have Wade Rycroft?"

I hear his chuckle as I turn the shower on.

My reflection actually makes me gasp. I look like shit. There's no other way to describe it. My hair is knotted, my eyes are completely bloodshot, and I look like I went a few rounds in a boxing ring with Tyson, based on the swelling.

How the hell am I going to look human enough to perform?

As much as I want to enjoy the shower, I don't have time. I quickly get myself scrubbed up, and thanks to the creep, I now get dressed in here.

I know the bus was swept for videos, but I'm completely sure whoever this guy is, he works on the tour in some capacity. Probably sound crew.

"Ten minutes, Emily." Wade's voice isn't condescending for the first time in his countdown.

I unlock the door and stare at him. "Why are you suddenly being nice?"

"Because you're listening."

"You're a complicated man."

He smiles. "Not really. I'm pretty simple. Tell me the truth, love your family, and do the right thing."

I sit at the table adjacent to him and the desire to tell him everything bubbles up. I've lied to everyone, and I no longer believe putting Cooper through this pain is the right thing.

My lips part, the words on the tip of my tongue, but they stay there. I don't tell him anything out of fear.

"And what about love?"

Wade shrugs. "Love is an illusion."

"Love is beautiful," I counter.

"Until you lose it."

There's nothing to say back to that. He's right. There's nothing beautiful about what I'm feeling right now. However, he isn't seeing the whole picture. "Even if I knew how this would go, I'd do it again and again. Because that beautiful part is worth all the ugly I'm feeling right now."

I grab my guitar and head to the stairs. Wade doesn't say anything as he follows, and I hope that one day some girl will show him that the reward is only there if you take a risk.

# Chapter Sixteen

Emily

Getting on stage was the hardest thing I ever did, but I'm here now.

Music transports me, gives me a sense of relief, and with all the feelings swirling around, I need a release. It's a gift that I feel my fans give me by allowing me the chance to give them a piece of me. Each song comes from deep in my soul.

"Would y'all mind if I sing something a little different tonight?"

Cheers erupt, and I strum my guitar and head to the edge of the stage. I sit with my legs over the side, and it's as if I'm with the crowd.

One of the stage crew brings a microphone to me. "Have you ever lost someone you loved?" I play a few chords. "I've had a rough few days, and I'd like to sing this song as if we're all sittin' in my living room. Tonight, you're my best friend and we're going to work out our pain. Is that all right?"

The crowd quiets, and there's only one song that fits this moment. I start the intro to my favorite Garth Brooks song. The lyrics to "The Dance" pour out of me. With my eyes closed, I imagine Cooper standing in front of me. I tell him how perfect my world was when I had him, and that even though things didn't work, I wouldn't change anything.

My voice is filled with my regret, my turmoil, and my anger toward the man who is doing this to me. I sing each note as if it could be my last and feel the tears that stream down my face.

I can almost see his green eyes as I give him this piece of my soul. Each verse speaks the truth regarding what's inside my heart.

When I finish, I open my eyes and the arena goes nuts. I see people wiping their faces, screaming with their hands in the air, and the clapping is deafening.

"Thank you for listenin'." I smile through the tears. "I love y'all so much!"

My throat is tight as I get to my feet. I walk back to center stage and pull myself together.

"All right, now I want everyone on their feet!" I shift gears and perform like it's my life's mission.

Song after song, I push past any performance I've ever given. The sounds coming from the audience let me know I did my job.

"Wow," Luke says as I head off the stage. "I've never seen anything like that."

"Thanks!" I bounce a little, feeding off the adrenaline.

"That was amazing!" Vince pulls me in his arms. "Damn, girl!"

Praises are passed around, and I blush a little. "Okay, y'all, it wasn't *that* great."

"Not that great?" Luke scoffs. "I don't want to follow that."

He's ridiculous. "I know you're just sayin' that because you know I'm feeling shitty."

Luke and Vince share a look and shake their heads. "No. We really aren't. That was impressive, and I have a feeling you won't be feeling shitty for very long if you keep that up."

I continue talking with the boys, but when they head out to stage, Wade escorts me back to the bus.

"Do you have my phone?" I ask.

He hands it to me, and my mood plummets when I note there's still no texts or calls.

"Have you talked to Cooper?" I ask, attempting to be indifferent.

"No. I figured after your breakup I'd hear something, but it's been two days and nothing."

The sound of my heartbeat pounds in my ears. "Nothin'?"

Cooper isn't a sit-back kind of guy, so I'm sort of shocked he didn't call Wade and lose his shit.

"Not a word. Made it easy to respect your wishes to keep him out of the loop."

I drop my eyes to the floor to hide my disappointment. "I guess I wasn't that important."

Or I hurt him so bad he can't stand the thought of me.

"You really have no idea how much he cares for you, do you?" Wade asks.

"Cared," I correct.

"Cares."

"You don't know the whole story. I assure you, there's no comin' back from it."

Wade smirks. "You know what drives a cowboy to go radio silent?"

"Pants too tight?"

He laughs and walks closer. "When he doesn't know how to handle feelin' out of control. I'm assuming it was you who ended it?"

I nod.

"And he was against it?"

"At first." *Right until I told him it was you who I had feelings for.*

Wade towers over me and sighs. "Until you pushed him to the brink?"

"Yeah," I admit.

"Well, he's probably pissed, but more than that, he doesn't know what to do about it. He'll figure it out, and when he does, darlin', I hope you're ready for what's comin'."

I have no idea what any of that means.

A knock on the door causes my heart to leap from my chest.

Wade walks over and steps outside. I can hear his voice raise but can't understand what he's saying. The other voices argue with him, and then he storms back into the bus, furious.

"Everything okay?" I ask, my throat dry as I wait for him to answer.

"I'm going to find this motherfucker," Wade says. "I'm going to tear him apart for what he's done."

"Done?" Fear grips me more than ever before as another possibility hits me. "Oh, God!" I sink down on the couch. "Please tell me…" Breathing is difficult as I gasp for air. I think about Cooper being hurt, or worse, because of me.

"Breathe, Emily." Wade's hands are on my shoulders. "I'm just upset."

"Is it Cooper?" I look at him, waiting for the worst.

Wade's warm brown eyes narrow. "Why would you think it's

Cooper?"

"I-I..." I stammer. "I just..."

He's crouched in front of me and takes my face in his hands.

"Why would that be what you thought?"

Before I can answer him, the door flies open and my world goes upside down.

# Chapter Seventeen

Cooper

Wade is holding her face as if he's going to kiss her.

"Get your hands off her," I say as I charge forward. I'm going to beat the shit out of him. Some fucking friend. "You son of a bitch!"

"Cooper!" Emily yells and moves in front of me. "Don't do this."

"What the hell is your problem?" Wade questions.

"You!" I bellow and push toward my target.

Emily tries to move me back, but there's no stopping me. I saw her tonight. I heard her sing that damn song, and I stupidly thought it was about us. Seems I was wrong... It was about her and Wade.

"Please! Calm down, Coop!" Emily yells, but there isn't a chance of that. "Please! It's not... It's not what you think."

Her small hands pull at my shoulders, but I'm heading toward him, ready to fight.

"Not what?" I laugh. "Not walking in on you and Wade in your intimate moment?"

"Intimate?" Wade slides back a step, casually leaning a shoulder against a wall as if I'm not two seconds away from ripping his throat out.

"At least give me the respect of admitting to whatever the two of you are doing." I shove closer.

Emily's fingers press against my face and she tilts my head down. "I lied, Cooper."

"Don't lie to me now, Emily. I saw you!"

She shakes her head. "No, I lied before. There's nothing goin' on."

"Can someone fill me in?" Wade's voice echoes in the small space.

Without taking her eyes from mine, Emily says, "I told Cooper I had feelings for you."

"You what?" His eyes dart between us. "Why the fuck would you say that?"

Emily takes a step back and wraps her arms around her stomach. "Because *he* told me I had to get rid of Cooper or he would!"

Wade clears his throat. "Who is he?"

"Him! Who do you think?"

"So that's why you pushed me away. Not because you have feelings for Wade?" I ask, the tight knot of rage loosening even though the hurt is still there.

"No! God, it isn't like that... I can't do this. I can't let him take you from me." Emily's voice cracks on the last word.

Her blue eyes lock on mine, and my anger dissipates a bit more. She's terrified, and her entire body is trembling. I step toward her, wanting to pull her into my arms and take away her fear. As much as I want that, I need to know what is going on.

"Wade?"

"Nothing is going on here, man." Wade gives me a look of incredulity, as if he can't believe I would actually buy that shit.

She shakes her head. "Cooper, you have to leave before he finds out you're here."

This time, I do pull her to me. "I'm not going anywhere."

Her head presses into my chest, and I feel her shake as she starts to sob.

"I'm not trying to interrupt, but when exactly did he, who I'm assuming is your stalker, make contact?" Wade presses for the answer I'd like to know as well.

"Two nights ago," she admits.

He moves closer, and my arms instinctually tighten. "I need you to tell me everything."

I help her to the couch, holding her the whole time. In my arms, Emily confesses everything about the other night. Her teeth chatter as she retells the details of things that were said.

All I want to do is find this guy and kill him myself. Not because of the cows—they're replaceable—but because he's terrified her. He's played games, hurt her, and made her feel as if she had to be alone in order for me to be safe.

I hold my emotions inside. She's been through enough, but if I ever come face to face with him, he'd better pray.

"What about his voice? Deep? Throaty? A lisp?"

She shakes her head and tries to describe his voice since he kept her from seeing his face. "His voice was low when he spoke, but he didn't have a twang or accent that I could tell."

"Okay, good. Keep going." Wade writes down things she says, nodding as she reveals another clue.

"His hands…" She shudders.

"He touched you?" I practically growl. I thought I knew what rage was before. I had no clue. He touched her, and for that alone, I'm going to kill him.

"You have nothing to be sorry about." Wade jumps in and shoots me a look. "If you need to step outside and cool off, go."

Like I'm going to leave her. "I'm fine."

Emily's hand squeezes mine.

"I'm sorry. You're doing great, darlin'," I encourage her. "What else did he say?"

She tells us more, and then Wade starts a new line of questioning.

"Was he taller than I am?"

"I don't know. He was big enough that I thought it was you." She pats her eyes with a tissue.

"Okay, I want you to close your eyes," Wade requests.

I see the panic of her pulse thrumming away on her neck. "We're right here, Emmy. No one is going to get near you."

Emily takes a few deep breaths and follows his instruction.

"Think about that night. Focus on your senses. Think about what you felt. Were his hands rough?"

"Yes." She shivers.

"Did his cheek touch yours? What was it like?"

"He was clean-shaven."

"Inhale and remember what you smelled. Anything you can tell me?"

Emily continues this way for a few more questions as she gives him more than I thought she ever would. Details that I can see him already starting to piece together.

"You did great, Em. I'm going to have people posted outside the door while I go to work." Wade's eyes meet mine, he dips his head, and walks toward the door.

We both stay quiet, the events of the last few days settling around us. Emily shifts to the side and then stands. "I know you hate me, but—"

"I don't hate you."

"You should."

"Because you thought I was going to die so you lied to me?" I get to my feet, and she retreats.

Emily rubs her forehead. "You've ignored me for two days. I didn't think I'd ever see you again."

She couldn't be more wrong. "I think me bein' here says otherwise."

Trent was right. I had two choices: fight for her or let her go.

"This is all too much, Cooper. It's too much."

"It doesn't have to be." I move quickly and gather her in my arms, holding her because I need to.

Emily's arms wrap around my waist as she clings to me. "The idea of him hurting you..."

"Isn't going to happen."

She looks up with concern etched on her perfect face. "I don't think you get it, Coop. When I got the first letter, I thought it was a joke. I didn't take it seriously, and we both know what happened. I wasn't willing to risk it a second time."

I run my finger down her cheek and graze her lips. "He can't have you. You're already taken."

She lets out a soft sigh. "I am?"

"You didn't think I'd really give up, did you?"

"I hoped you wouldn't..."

This woman owns my heart, and I'm perfectly fine with never getting it back.

"You don't have to hope. I'll fight through whatever obstacles we encounter. I know you thought you were doing what you had to, but I'm not going anywhere."

Emily's lip trembles. "If he hurts you, then what?"

I shrug. "I'm not worried about me."

Her arms drop, and she pulls away. "You didn't hear him tell you his delusional ideas about me and him. I had to stand there and listen to him talk about killing you." Emily's voice drops to a whisper. "He listens. He watches. He's not going to give up either."

There's nothing saying her fear isn't valid, but I'm not afraid. "Not a chance in hell I'm going to walk away and let some piece of shit torment you." I grip her wrist. "Do you love me?"

"Yes."

The single word melts the last two days of frustration.

"Do you trust me?" I ask.

"Yes."

I push my hands up into her hair and bring our faces together. "Then show me."

Emily grips my neck and pushes up on her toes. Her lips press against mine. It's been weeks since I've felt her touch, and after everything in the last few days, I need her.

My tongue glides against hers as I thread my fingers through her hair, tightening slightly. She kisses me harder, deeper.

I want to take it all away from her. Make her forget everything else but us. I push her back against the wall, pinning her with my hips. She moans, and I tilt her head to the side to get better access. I move my hand down her throat and across her shoulder. I've missed her skin. I've missed everything about her.

My lips travel the path that my fingers made, and she sighs.

I love the noises she makes.

I'm so lost in the moment I don't hear anyone enter the bus or notice anyone's presence until Emily pulls back and terror fills her eyes. "No!"

Cold metal touches my neck, and I know one of us isn't going to make it out of here.

# Chapter Eighteen

Emily

Cooper doesn't move a muscle. He shields me as I stare into the eyes of one of Luke's bodyguards. I've seen him a few times, but he's one of the rovers. I don't remember his name even though Luke pointed him out a few times.

I look over Cooper's shoulder. "It's okay, this is my boyfriend. You can put the gun down. I'm totally fine."

Instead of lowering the gun pointed at Cooper's neck, he pushes the barrel deeper.

"Did you hear me?" I ask, shifting a little, but Cooper won't move his arms.

"I heard you just fine." His voice fills the air, and my blood runs cold. This voice has haunted my every waking minute for the last two days.

"Don't move." Cooper looks in my eyes, telling me more than just his words. "Stay exactly where you are."

I see his fear and worry as we stand here completely at a crazy person's mercy.

"Your boyfriend?" He laughs. "You really are a dumb bitch."

Cooper tenses a little more but doesn't say a word. He watches me, covering me with his body, protecting me even though he's the one with a gun pressed to his throat. My heart races, and once again, I know I need to keep this guy talking. If I can control the situation, get him to relax, maybe Wade will get back and we can all make it out of here.

"I know you're angry," I say quickly. "I'm sorry. I ended things, just like I promised. I waited two days for you." I try to put as much energy as I can muster into my lie, digging deep to give an epic performance.

My hope is that I can get him to think my depression was because he never came for me, so he'll calm down.

Wade's voice comes over the two-way radio. "Brookes, is the perimeter clear? I can't find the other guard."

He brings the radio to his mouth. "All clear here, boss. The package hasn't left the building."

"Keep an eye out until I find the other guard. We need to ensure Emily's safety."

"I'll handle it," Brookes promises. He cracks his neck and moves so he's closer to me. "Now that we have a little more time, why don't you tell your *boyfriend* here all about the games you've been playing."

"I'm not playing any games, Brookes." I use his name for the first time, and his eyes light up. "I waited for two days for you to come around, but you didn't. I thought you didn't love me, and I was broken and alone."

Brookes relaxes just slightly, but it's a start. "Yet, you wouldn't let me in..."

"You never came for me." I try to move, but Cooper lowers his arm so I can't.

All I want is to get the gun off his neck. Brookes is unstable, but if he's going to shoot anyone first, it'll be Cooper. I won't allow that to happen.

Brookes doesn't say anything more. His eyes go back to Cooper as if he forgot he was in the room. "Why don't we ask Cooper what he thinks of his girlfriend sneaking around behind his back? Maybe he'll finally see that you don't love him and he was a fool to come here."

I let my lip tremble and will my face to melt into a mask of sadness and hurt. "You want us to have a chance, but you left me, and now you have a gun pointed at me. I thought you loved me."

*Come on. Where are the tears when I need them?*

He flinches. "It's pointed at *him*! He's standing in our way, Emily."

"If you love me, you wouldn't want to hurt me."

Cooper's eyes meet mine, and we tell each other everything in our gazes. He's scared, he loves me, and he's going to go down protecting me.

I move my hand slightly, touching his hip, needing to be as close to him as possible.

His lip lifts a small amount, and he clears his throat. "Listen, Brookes, right?"

The sound of Cooper's voice causes his eyes to blaze. My fear spikes, wanting Cooper to just follow my lead.

"I get it, you love her, and she's been playing the both of us. I'd be pissed, too. Hell, I am pissed. I don't understand how the hell she could think this is fucking cool."

Brookes's eyes shift from Cooper to me, and his head bobs a little in agreement. "It's why I'm so confused."

"I'm right there with you." Cooper shakes his head in disappointment. "If I knew you guys were this serious, I would've backed off." He tilts to look at Brookes. "It's the bro code and all."

Brookes looks at me and huffs. "It could've been so easy."

"I'm sorry. I didn't know." I pretend to be full of sorrow. "I thought..."

Cooper moves slightly, urging me to the side a little. "I know you love Emily."

"She's all I think about," Brookes admits, and I fight back the urge to puke. "I thought she loved me. She's a lying whore."

This is the most insane conversation ever. He needs serious mental help. There's no way a sane person would think after meeting *maybe* four times that we would be in love. Not to mention, I've only spoken to him one time.

"I'm going to turn around so we can talk man to man, okay?"

"Don't fucking try anything."

Cooper raises his hands as Brookes keeps the gun pointed at him. "I'm not stupid, man." His back is to my front, and he still shields me from the lunatic before us. "I'm more than willing to step out of the way so you guys can be together, but you have to think about this...if you kill me in front of her, how will she ever be okay after? You know her, she hates blood."

Brookes looks to me, and I nod.

"Let Emily go, and we'll work this out, okay?"

My hands grip Cooper's shirt. There's no way in hell I'm letting him stay here alone. It ain't happening.

Confliction paints Brookes's face. He drops the gun slightly, and I feel a tinge of hope.

Cooper's hands fall, he pushes my hip to the side, and we move so I now have a clear way to the door. He's sadly mistaken if he thinks I'm going anywhere without him.

"Tell me, have you known Emily long?" Cooper urges.

"Long enough to know we're meant to be."

"When you know, you know, right?"

"I'm done with this conversation. She either leaves or I end this with her here," Brookes warns.

"Em," Coop says. "You need to go outside."

I dig my nails in his back and tears pool. "Please don't do this, Brookes. Please!" I plead. "If you love me, you won't hurt me like this. You won't make me live with knowing I'm responsible."

I can't move my legs. I can't do this. I don't know what the hell Cooper is thinking, but Wade should be back any minute. He'll know what to do.

Brookes looks at me as the tears fall freely. I'm not pretending anymore, I'm truly terrified and broken by the idea of walking out that door.

He sighs, drops his hand more, and before I have a chance to blink, Cooper lunges.

# Chapter Nineteen

Emily

Time doesn't slow when you think you're going to die. I don't know who the hell says they're hyper aware because nothing is registering right now. I can't see whose hands are where. I can't decipher who is making what noises. All I see are limbs moving and punches landing. Brookes and Cooper battle. I stand in horror, not knowing if Cooper is hurt or where the gun is.

I hear Cooper grunt, and the sound of cracking turns my stomach. "Cooper!" Tears fill my vision as I see his head fall to the side.

"Go, Emily! Run!" he yells, but I can't walk away from him.

"I'm not leaving you!" I cry out.

I have to help him. Brookes lands another punch, but Cooper fights back.

*Where the fuck is Wade?*

Then I remember my panic button.

I turn and dive for it. I press the red button, knowing the alarm will blare out to the whole security team.

Sure enough, Brookes's radio shrieks.

"Fuck you!" Brookes says as he hits Coop again.

"I'll fucking kill you for touchin' her!" Cooper replies, and my eyes catch the reflection off the shiny metal barrel that was lost in the scuffle.

I move forward and grip the handle. "Stop!" I scream pointing the gun at them. "Stop moving or I'll shoot!"

Both men go still.

Brookes looks up and fear fills his gaze. "Baby."

"I'm not your baby. I don't even know you, but you've tormented me for weeks. You've made my life miserable, and now you tried to kill the man I love. So don't you dare speak to me. Get up!" I nudge the muzzle upward, indicating he needs to stand.

He obeys, and then Cooper lands a punch on his face, blood sprays, and I scream.

He hits him again and again, until Brookes's body goes limp.

My gun is still pointed, and my hands begin to shake. I'm standing here, but emotionally, I'm gone.

Then he's in front of me, his skin warm as his fingers gently wrap around my wrist, slowly lowering the weapon.

"Em?" His voice is soft.

My eyes meet his, but I still don't speak.

"Darlin', I need you to go get Wade," Cooper instructs me. "I'll hold him."

I stand, looking at Cooper with blood on his shirt.

"I'm okay, Emily. It's over now."

Will this ever really be over?

Before I can even breathe, the door opens, and Wade is the first person through, gun raised. He grabs me, pushing me behind him. A different bodyguard lifts me and pivots to take me down the steps, but as soon as I can't see Cooper, I snap. My arms flail as I fight against his hold. "Let me go!" I claw my way out of his arms.

I don't trust any of these people. Strength I never knew I had flows through me, and I manage to push my way out of his grasp. "Cooper! Wade!" I scream and move toward them.

"It's fine, let her go." Wade holsters his weapon, and I position myself behind him. "Are you okay?" he asks.

"Yes. No. I don't really know."

He turns to Cooper, and his voice is hard. "What the fuck? Brookes? Are you... Un-fucking-real," Wade says as he crouches down.

"A little help?" Cooper huffs as he shifts his weight and Brookes starts to wake.

"Man, you get all the fun." Wade huffs and drops to his knees to secure Brookes's wrists in a set of handcuffs.

Cooper shakes his head and laughs. "Nice of you to show up."

"Next time, don't start the party early. It's not my fault I was out looking for the guy while you were supposed to be keeping her occupied."

"I was trying until your psycho friend came in with a gun."

Wade brushes his dark hair back and scratches his neck. "Cock blocked by your girl's stalker. Bad timing."

"Are you two serious?" I ask in complete shock. I can't believe these two are joking about a party when two minutes ago Cooper was being attacked and had a gun to his head—literally.

"Get him the hell out of here and call the police to come get him," Wade orders the guy who tried to carry me off the bus.

Cooper's eyes meet mine as he wipes the blood from his hands. I focus on the tiny speckles of dark green against the lighter shades, and my heart races. He saved our lives. In so many ways, he's my savior. I've waited my entire life for someone to love me enough, and here he is.

Two hours later, after statements, police questioning, and retelling the horror story we just lived, everything is quiet. Brookes is going to jail, and thanks to the cameras Wade had installed, everything is on tape. Wade and the guys have cleaned the bus back up, but I'm not staying in it again, no matter how much anyone pays me.

Wade walks us to the hotel door, much more relaxed than I've ever seen him. "You guys all right?"

"We're going to be fine now that it's over," Cooper says to Wade, but he watches me.

I give him a soft smile. "Thank you," I say, touching Wade's arm. "Thank you for everything."

"It was my pleasure."

As resistant as I had been to Wade, he's become my friend as well. He's kind, funny, bossy as all hell, but has a heart hidden under all his tough exterior.

"I'm actually going to miss you." I laugh. "You better find a good woman who will take care of you."

He laughs with his whole body. "Last thing I need is a woman."

Cooper's arm wraps around my shoulders, tucking me in to his side. "You'll change your mind."

Wade rolls his eyes. "Not many girls want a battered ex-Green Beret who doesn't like insubordination."

I move out of Cooper's arms and pull Wade into a hug. "You're not battered. You're a good man, Wade Rycroft. Don't sell yourself short." My fingers press against his cheek, and he grins.

"You be good to him." He lifts his chin toward Cooper.

"I will."

He pulls me to his chest and kisses the top of my head. "Freaking women."

Cooper claps his hand in Wade's, and they give a man version of a hug. "Be careful and don't be a stranger."

I move back to Cooper, wrapping my arms around his middle. We watch Wade get in his pickup truck, and I wave goodbye, hoping we'll see him soon.

# Chapter Twenty

Emily

We enter the room, both remaining silent for several minutes. My arms stay around him, needing him to anchor me.

This nightmare is finally over.

The shock of everything comes crashing around me as we stand here alone in the room, looking at each other. He could've died. I would've seen the only man I've ever loved taken from this earth. All because that psycho was living in some twisted version of reality.

"You almost…" I whisper as I shake my head, taking a step back. "You could've—"

He looks at me as I struggle to keep from breaking down. Instead of falling apart, I fall into Cooper's arms, and he holds me tight. "It's okay, Emmy. It's okay."

"I almost lost you."

"You didn't. I'm right here."

A part of my brain won't allow me to believe that we're both okay. I lean back so I can touch his face, his hair, his chest, checking to make sure he's really here and alive. My fingers trace the bruise that's starting to form as a tear falls from my eyes. "He hurt you."

"Not in a way that won't heal." Cooper wipes my cheek and cups my face. "Don't cry, darlin'."

"If he had killed you—"

Cooper hushes me by bringing his lips to mine. He kisses me tenderly, and my hands move up his shoulders, his neck, and to the back of his head, needing to stay like this. We kiss each other, emotions taking over.

His hands skim down my back until he's gripping my thighs, pulling me into his arms. "I need you."

"I need you, too," I reply anxiously.

It isn't wanting at this point. It's a physical ache that only he can soothe.

"I have to love you," he explains almost frantically.

"Please. Make love to me."

He moves us back to the bed and places me down gently. I take in his dark brown hair, the stubble on his cheeks, and the passion in his eyes as he braces over me. I'm a lucky woman.

As we come face to face, my breath is taken away when I see a lone tear start to fall.

My fingers capture the bead and neither of us speak.

Sometimes words aren't needed.

Sometimes silence says it all.

Our lips collide, and I lose myself in his touch. His tongue moves against mine, and I moan. Everything that's happened the last few weeks disappears as he kisses me.

His hand moves down my chest, brushing his thumb against my nipple. He leans up, removes his shirt, and then tears mine off. The heat in his eyes burns my skin as my shorts and bra follow.

He can't move fast enough.

"Don't make me wait," I plead.

"Never."

Cooper's tongue licks around the peak of my nipple, and my head falls back. I grip the back of his head as he sucks and then his teeth bite down while he slips a finger in my pussy. I nearly buck off the bed, but Cooper keeps me where he wants me.

"Tell me you're mine," Cooper demands as he pushes another finger in.

"Only yours!"

He pumps in and out, and I climb higher. I don't know if it's the remaining adrenaline that lingers, but I'm on fire. He ignites the flame, causing me to burn from the inside out. I need him—all of him.

"Cooper," I cry out as my orgasm teeters. "I need you! Now!"

He removes his pants and climbs back into place. Our eyes meet as he slowly enters me.

Bliss. It's complete and total bliss.

I'm filled in every possible way. My heart is full of love for this man. Everything in my world makes sense this very instant. I never want to lose this. I'll do everything I can to hold on to what we have.

Cooper completes the missing piece of my heart.

"I love you. I love you. I love you so much." I can't hold in my feelings. If I try, they will shred me from the inside just to get out.

He slows his pace, kisses my lips, and smiles. "I love you. Don't ever try to leave me again."

My fingers dig into his back, keeping him as close as possible. "You never have to worry about that."

We make love. Losing ourselves and all understanding of time. I don't think about anything other than us while we're in each other's arms. I'm able to breathe when he's around.

After, when we're both sated and panting softly, I lie on his chest, listening to the steady thrum of his heart. My finger makes random patterns on his stomach, and his hand rests on my hip.

"Why didn't you just tell me?" he asks after a long while of comfortable silence.

I turn my head to face him. "I was scared he'd kill you. I was willing to end our relationship if it meant that you were safe."

He releases a heavy sigh. "God willing there's never a next time, but if there is, just talk to me. We would've figured something out."

Hurting Cooper was the last thing I wanted to do. I hated every second of knowing he was upset. "I'm sorry I lied. I'm even more sorry I made you think there was another man."

It was the worst thing I could've said. Cooper has been someone's second choice each time he's given a girl a chance. Both of us have had shit luck until we finally found our way together. I believe we had to drudge ourselves through the mucky water to find our way to the clear springs.

"I've been waiting my whole life to feel the way I feel with you. I'm crazy about you, and there's no way I was going to lose you."

I smile, bring the tip of my finger to his cheek, and run it against his stubble. "Who would've thought two kids from the opposite side of the tracks would fall in love all these years later?"

His hand wraps around my fingers. "Especially since you were right under my nose the whole time."

"I was just waitin' for you to finally ask me out."

That isn't completely true, but Cooper was definitely someone I considered. I wasn't really sure of what my feelings were for him, so I sank into music instead of finding out. He is a friend and a good man—he always has been, yet my goal had always been to get out of Bell Buckle.

Here I am now wanting to go home...to Cooper.

"Well, you have me now."

I grin. "I sure do, and you're stuck with me."

"Yeah? Is that so?" Cooper's hands grip my arms, and he lifts me so we're nose to nose.

"Yup."

His lips touch mine, and I melt. "For how long?"

"How long do you want me?" I ask playfully.

"Marry me."

I gasp, looking down at him with wide eyes. "What?"

Cooper sits up, taking me with him. "Marry me. I want you to marry me."

My mouth opens and closes like a fish. "Are you... It's so soon... And we just went through all that. Are you sure? Do you really want this?"

He cups my face in his hands, eyes dancing back and forth between mine as I watch without blinking. "I love you. I'll be good to you. And I'll make you happy. There's nothing I want more, and I'm completely sure. Will you be my wife?"

My heart races as I try to find the words that have escaped me. It's crazy, impulsive, and I love him. I know there is no one else in the world I want to be with, and every excuse that rolls around my head seems trivial.

"Yes!" The word flies from my lips as I wrap my arms around him.

Only Cooper could take the darkest day and turn it bright. He chases away the clouds, keeps the storms at bay, and allows me to dance in his rays.

# Epilogue

~Three Years Later~

Cooper

"Emily!" I call for my wife from the music studio I had installed right after the wedding.

"Coming, honey! I'm just finishing this song."

We're going to be late, but I know better than to push her out of there. She'll spend an hour fretting that she'll forget the word or note, then another hour repeating it so she doesn't forget, and then God knows how long telling me how she isn't sure she remembered it.

It's a process, and I've learned to let her have it.

Sure enough, it takes her ten more minutes to emerge.

"Sorry!" She lifts her shoulders and gives me an impish smile.

"It's fine." I kiss the side of her head. "We have a half hour."

"What?" Emily squeaks and slaps my chest. "I have more time?"

I shake my head. "No. We have to go sign the papers."

Emily sighs and tears fill her blue eyes. "What if—"

"No." I stop her right there. I know where she's going with this, and I won't let her go down this road again. The last three years have been filled with a lot of changes, most good, but this has been the scariest.

Emily and I immediately tried for a family. She wanted a child, but I couldn't give her one. After three failed pregnancies, we decided to adopt.

I look down at our newborn baby girl in her car seat, and my heart swells. Today, Mia officially becomes our daughter.

"I need to prepare, Cooper. I can't lose her." Emily squats and runs gentle fingertips over our daughter's tiny hand.

"We're not losing her, darlin'." I will the words to be true. It's been five days that we've had her, and there's no way to explain the love I have for this little girl.

She owns me.

Emily looks up with wet lashes. "I love her so much."

"I love both my girls, and I'm not letting go of either."

Her eyes go back to Mia and she kisses her chubby cheek. "Did you hear that, princess? Your daddy loves us."

I crouch down, placing my hand on Emily's back. "Let's go make her ours."

Emily's lip trembles slightly, but she nods and looks away.

The ride to the courthouse is quiet. I may seem sure of myself, but it's only for Emily. Inside, I'm terrified. The mere idea of someone taking her away from us makes me want to fall apart. Mia became mine the minute they placed her in my arms. I thought I fell in love with my wife instantly, but it was nothing like holding my little girl.

"Did your mama say she was comin' by today?" Emily asks.

"Presley and Mama said they'd be there when we got home," I say as I glance over at her.

"I think Grace and Angie, too."

I nod. I know no matter which way this goes, we will want our family and friends. She has no idea, but there will be a lot more people than she thinks. Papa always said to prepare for the outcome you want, so I did. When we get home, there will be a big group waiting to celebrate the official adoption of Mia Ryann Townsend.

I take her hand in mine and squeeze. "It'll be fine, darlin'."

Emily drops her head to my shoulder. "I just want this over with so I can breathe again."

There's nothing either of us can say to ease the other. Instead of trying to sway her, I'm just here with her. I take comfort from her touch and feel her tense when we park.

"No matter what, we'll fight for her, okay?" I look at Emily and promise to do what I can.

"Okay."

We grab the baby from the backseat and walk inside. Our lawyer leads us to the bench in the hallway and explains the process again. I don't hear much that he says. My mind starts to play various possibilities, all of which make my stomach clench.

Emily wraps her arm around mine, and we both stare down at Mia. I can feel the nerves rolling off her and hear her sniff. If I could take this from her, I would. My heart pounds against my chest as I see our lawyer emerge from the conference room where we'll hopefully sign the papers.

"Come on back," he says stoically.

The fear in my wife's eyes stirs my protectiveness. "Coop?"

I grab my lawyer's arm as he's walking away. "Russ? Is she going to sign?"

"I don't know because she has up until the last second to change her mind. The longer we give her to think..." Russ explains, and I nod.

My eyes meet Emily's, and I force a smile. "I'll never let go of her, just like I wouldn't you. Trust me?"

A tear drops. "Yes."

"I love you."

"I love you."

We walk the fifty feet into the room to see the Mia's birth mother, Darlene, clutching her stomach. Tears fall from her eyes, and I can see the heartbreak across her face. She may only be sixteen, but right now, she looks much older.

The judge explains the details of the adoption and allows a chance for questions. Darlene asks if she can say something, which he allows.

Emily's hand clenches mine, and her body shakes slightly.

Darlene wipes her face and looks between us. "I know you'll give her the life she deserves. I wish I could be the mama she needs, but I can't. I hate the idea of givin' her up, but I know it's the right thing—" She sobs and then manages, "If she ever asks about me, will you tell her I loved her and that's why I let her go?"

Emily is out of her seat and pulling the young girl in her arms. They both cry, holding on to each other. "I'll tell her how brave you are. I'll tell her how strong you are. I'll tell her how her beauty comes from you," Emily promises. "I'll love her for the both of us. She'll have two mamas who will always do what's right for her."

She nods. "I'm ready."

Darlene signs the papers, and it's official. Mia is our daughter.

When she leaves the room, Emily bursts into tears, only this time, they are from joy.

* * * *

"Congratulations!" the room erupts with shouts and cheers and applause as we walk in.

Emily gives me a smirk and laughs. "I can't believe you."

"We needed to officially welcome Mia to our crazy clan." I nudge her.

Our family rushes forward, giving hugs and gushing over our daughter.

"Welcome to fatherhood." Wyatt chuckles. "Girls are a whole different world, man. They're scary as hell. And she's about to be five."

Wyatt's little girl is a handful, but it isn't surprising considering she's a Hennington and the first granddaughter. His mama spoils the shit out of her, and they're paying for it now.

"I'm glad to be in the fatherhood club."

He grins and slaps my shoulder. "I'm glad you are, too. You know, between Felicity, Hannah, and now Mia, we've basically created a whole new generation of our childhood," Wyatt muses.

"I really hope Trent is retired by the time they hit their teens."

"Right? Can you see him having to pick up his nieces and daughter?"

We both laugh.

Trent walks over and lifts his chin. "What's so funny?"

Wyatt tells him what we were joking about, and his face falls.

"How the hell are you two laughing? I'll be callin' your asses to get them out of jail."

"Let's just hope they're nothing like their mamas," I say, not wanting to think of my daughter and jail at all.

He bobs his head up and down. "Especially with the boy crap. I'm not even going to entertain some little shit cowboy trying to date my daughter."

"Damn right," I agree.

"We know what their little pea brains are thinkin' about," Trent adds.

Don't we ever.

"So, we're in agreement to beat any little grabby bastard who comes near our girls?" I ask.

"Yup," they both say in unison.

"Deal."

"Well, look what the cat dragged in." I smile and clap Wade's hand as we shake.

He smirks. "I figured you might need someone to come kick your ass since Emily said you were being a jerk."

I don't believe him for a second. If anything, I've been giving her whatever she wants to keep her calm. Adopting Mia was scary as hell. She's this beautiful baby that needed us, but we were terrified to love her and lose her.

"Wade!" Emily screams and rushes toward him.

"Shit," he grumbles.

"Come meet your goddaughter." Emily winks at me and then she's dragging him away.

We thought it was only natural that Wade be somewhat of a protector of Mia. He's the reason we're together. I owe him everything.

Zach walks over after extracting himself from a conversation with my father. "Thanks for saving me," he jokes.

Since retirement, my father is a world of fun. He's getting older, and I'm pretty sure Mama drives him crazy. His whole life was spent working on the farm, and now he gets to listen to her stories all day. He practically begs to come hide at my house.

"He's just tryin' to keep Mama and her friends from talkin' to him."

"The older they get, the worse they are," Trent notes.

Our mothers are all best friends and the world's biggest meddlers. Sometimes they use their powers for good, other times...not. They also like to take credit for anything they can. If you ask them, they're the reason we're all married. Not that we played a part in it—it was all them.

"Look at this." Presley smiles. "The Hennington and Townsend troublemakers all together."

My sister should talk. "Because your group was so innocent?"

She rolls her eyes. "We were following your lead."

Zach laughs. "Right. I love you, but you're crazy." He wraps his arms around her, resting his head on her shoulder. She visibly relaxes just being around Zach. It makes me happy seeing her so content.

"Cayden and Logan here?" I ask. I haven't seen my nephews. Then again, they're at the age where they're chasing the girls.

"They will be. They both have baseball and then Logan needs to walk his girlfriend home," Presley explains. "Another thing for me to worry about..."

"What?" Wyatt asks.

"Them havin' sex." She shudders.

To me, the boys are still eleven-year-olds coming to the farm for the first time, but they're the same age as the girl who just gave us Mia. Scary to think this baby could've come from my nephews. Time moves so fast, and if you blink, life can pass you by.

"You were their age," Trent reminds her.

"Shut up. I was a good girl."

He shrugs as Zach bursts out laughing. "Baby, you were *very* good."

"Gross, man. That's my sister."

The party continues for a while until all our parents head out. We head back to the deck where the kids are running around, chasing chickens, and I'm reminded life is good.

For a long time, I wasn't sure I'd marry, have kids, or be anything more than a rancher, and here I stand with everything and more.

I glance at Emily with Mia in her arms. A love so intense that it takes my breath away washes over me.

My feet move toward them, and I kiss them both. "What was that for?" Emily asks with a soft smile.

"I'm just happy," I tell her.

Her eyes brighten. "Yeah? Why is that?"

There is no shortage of reasons, but I choose the ones that I know will make her smile.

"Let's see. I have the most gorgeous and talented wife."

Emily grins. "Good reason."

"She is about to win a Grammy for the song about how perfect I am." I nudge her.

She giggles. "Was it? I thought it was about someone else..."

Yeah, right. "Nice try."

"We both know you're my world." She bats her eyelashes. "What else are you happy about?"

My throat goes dry, and it becomes hard to speak. "That we can hold on to her forever."

"We don't have to let go," she says with tears in her eyes.

Emily lifts Mia up on her shoulder before pressing her lips to her head. My hand rests on Mia's back, and I kiss my wife. "No, darlin'. We sure don't."

THE END

Sign up for the 1001 Dark Nights Newsletter
and be entered to win a Tiffany Lock necklace.

There's a contest every quarter!

Go to www.1001DarkNights.com for more information.

As a bonus, all subscribers will receive a free copy of
*Discovery Bundle Three*
Featuring stories by
Sidney Bristol, Darcy Burke, T. Gephart
Stacey Kennedy, Adriana Locke
JB Salsbury, and Erika Wilde

# Discover the Lexi Blake Crossover Collection

*Available now!*

Close Cover by Lexi Blake

Remy Guidry doesn't do relationships. He tried the marriage thing once, back in Louisiana, and learned the hard way that all he really needs in life is a cold beer, some good friends, and the occasional hookup. His job as a bodyguard with McKay-Taggart gives him purpose and lovely perks, like access to Sanctum. The last thing he needs in his life is a woman with stars in her eyes and babies in her future.

Lisa Daley's life is finally going in the right direction. She has finally graduated from college after years of putting herself through school. She's got a new job at an accounting firm and she's finished her Sanctum training. Finally on her own and having fun, her life seems pretty perfect. Except she's lonely and the one man she wants won't give her a second look.

There is one other little glitch. Apparently, her new firm is really a front for the mob and now they want her dead. Assassins can really ruin a fun girls' night out. Suddenly strapped to the very same six-foot-five-inch hunk of a bodyguard who makes her heart pound, Lisa can't decide if this situation is a blessing or a curse.

As the mob closes in, Remy takes his tempting new charge back to the safest place he knows—his home in the bayou. Surrounded by his past, he can't help wondering if Lisa is his future. To answer that question, he just has to keep her alive.

\* \* \* \*

Her Guardian Angel by Larissa Ione

After a difficult childhood and a turbulent stint in the military, Declan Burke finally got his act together. Now he's a battle-hardened professional bodyguard who takes his job at McKay-Taggart seriously and his playtime – and his play*mates* – just as seriously. One thing he never does, however, is mix business with pleasure. But when the mysterious, gorgeous Suzanne D'Angelo needs his protection from a stalker, his desire for her burns out of control, tempting him to break all the rules…even as he's drawn into a dark, dangerous world he didn't know existed.

Suzanne is an earthbound angel on her critical first mission: protecting Declan from an emerging supernatural threat at all costs. To keep him close, she hires him as her bodyguard. It doesn't take long for her to realize that she's in over her head, defenseless against this devastatingly sexy human who makes her crave his forbidden touch.

Together they'll have to draw on every ounce of their collective training to resist each other as the enemy closes in, but soon it becomes apparent that nothing could have prepared them for the menace to their lives…or their hearts.

* * * *

Justify Me by J. Kenner

McKay-Taggart operative Riley Blade has no intention of returning to Los Angeles after his brief stint as a consultant on mega-star Lyle Tarpin's latest action flick. Not even for Natasha Black, Tarpin's sexy personal assistant who'd gotten under his skin. Why would he, when Tasha made it absolutely clear that—attraction or not—she wasn't interested in a fling, much less a relationship.

But when Riley learns that someone is stalking her, he races to her side. Determined to not only protect her, but to convince her that—no matter what has hurt her in the past—he's not only going to fight for her, he's going to win her heart. Forever.

* * * *

Say You Won't Let Go by Corinne Michaels

I've had two goals my entire life:
1. Make it big in country music.
2. Get the hell out of Bell Buckle.

I was doing it. I was on my way, until Cooper Townsend landed backstage at my show in Dallas.

This gorgeous, rugged, man of few words was one cowboy I couldn't afford to let distract me. But with his slow smile and rough hands, I just couldn't keep away.

Now, there are outside forces conspiring against us. Maybe we should've known better? Maybe not. Even with the protection from Wade Rycroft, bodyguard for McKay-Taggart, I still don't feel safe. I won't let him get hurt because of me. All I know is that I want to hold on, but know the right thing to do is to let go...

\* \* \* \*

His to Protect by Carly Phillips

Talia Shaw has spent her adult life working as a scientist for a big pharmaceutical company. She's focused on saving lives, not living life. When her lab is broken into and it's clear someone is after the top secret formula she's working on, she turns to the one man she can trust. The same irresistible man she turned away years earlier because she was too young and naive to believe a sexy guy like Shane Landon could want *her*.

Shane Landon's bodyguard work for McKay-Taggart is the one thing that brings him satisfaction in his life. Relationships come in second to the job. Always. Then little brainiac Talia Shaw shows up in his backyard, frightened and on the run, and his world is turned upside down. And not just because she's found him naked in his outdoor shower, either.

With Talia's life in danger, Shane has to get her out of town and to her eccentric, hermit mentor who has the final piece of the formula she's been working on, while keeping her safe from the men who are after her. Guarding Talia's body certainly isn't any hardship, but he never expects to fall hard and fast for his best friend's little sister and the only woman who's ever really gotten under his skin.

* * * *

Rescuing Sadie by Susan Stoker

Sadie Jennings was used to being protected. As the niece of Sean Taggart, and the receptionist at McKay-Taggart Group, she was constantly surrounded by Alpha men more than capable, and willing, to lay down their life for her. But when she visits her friend in San Antonio, and acts on suspicious activity at Milena's workplace, Sadie puts both of them in the crosshairs of a madman. After several harrowing weeks, her friend is now safe, but for Sadie, the repercussions of her rash act linger on.

Chase Jackson, no stranger to dangerous situations as a captain in the US Army, has volunteered himself as Sadie's bodyguard. He fell head over heels for the beautiful woman the first time he laid eyes on her. With a Delta Force team at his back, he reassures the Taggart's that Sadie will be safe. But when the situation in San Antonio catches up with her, Chase has to use everything he's learned over his career to keep his promise...and to keep Sadie alive long enough to officially make her his.

# About Corinne Michaels

New York Times, USA Today, and Wall Street Journal Bestseller Corinne Michaels is the author of nine romance novels. She's an emotional, witty, sarcastic, and fun-loving mom of two beautiful children. Corinne is happily married to the man of her dreams and is a former Navy wife.

After spending months away from her husband while he was deployed, reading and writing was her escape from the loneliness. She enjoys putting her characters through intense heartbreak and finding a way to heal them through their struggles. Her stories are chock full of emotion, humor, and unrelenting love.

# One Last Time
By Corinne Michaels
Now Available

*From New York Times bestselling author, Corinne Michaels, comes a new heartwarming standalone romance.*

I'm getting really good at cutting my losses.

First, the husband. Divorcing him was the best decision I ever made. But between single-parenting and job-hunting, I can't catch my breath. When a celebrity blogging position falls into my lap, I'm determined to succeed.

That is, until I get my first assignment and actually see Noah Frazier for the first time...practically naked and dripping wet. My heart races and I forget how to form complete sentences. His chiseled abs, irresistible smirk, and crystal blue eyes are too perfect to be real. So, what do I do? Get drunk and humiliate myself, of course.

I'm ready to forget the awkward night, yet Noah has no intention of allowing me to move on. Instead, he arranges for me to write a feature on him, ensuring a lot more time together. One embarrassing moment after another, one kiss after another, and before I can stop myself, I realize—I'm falling in love with him.

But when the unthinkable happens, can I even blame him for cutting his losses?

What I wouldn't give for just one last time...

\* \* \* \*

Standing on the edge of the pool is the most gorgeous male specimen I've ever seen. The photo of Noah Frazier is absolutely nothing compared to the living version. He's taller than I imagined with a wide frame and tanned skin. His hair is wet, appearing almost black, and little drops of water fall from the tips, sliding down his perfect body. I watch the rivulets slide from his chest and then lower as they follow the ridges of his six-pack.

I grip the counter to stop from falling over. "Oh my God," I say, barely breathing the words.

Heather's head twists, and when she looks back at me, her grin is wide. "Yeah, God definitely made them."

"I can't go out there," I stammer. "I'll never be able to speak."

There is not a chance in hell I won't make a total fool of myself.

"You have to!" Heather grips my hand. "He's expecting a reporter friend to interview him."

My stomach drops. No, no, no, she didn't.

"You told him?" I scream the question.

She laughs and drains her glass. "Of course we did. Trust me, it's better he knows. We explained you're one of my best friends and that you wanted to talk for a bit. Eli said he was more than happy to do the interview for you."

Jesus. I'm going to kill her.

I grab my drink and throw it back. My throat burns, and I cough as the warmth starts to flow through my veins.

"Easy!" She warns while slapping my back.

"This is going to be so embarrassing," I whine.

Heather laughs as she pours another drink. "Yup. Yup it is, but oh so entertaining."

Maybe I can duck back out and no one will ever know. There's nothing saying I have to do this. My boss is, like, twelve, I'm sure I can come up with something plausible. Celebrities aren't known for being reliable.

Ugh.

I need this job, though.

Before I can make a move either way, the glass door slides open and Noah walks through the threshold.

My legs start to quiver as his eyes meet mine. All I can think about is how I'd like to climb him like a tree and shake his coconuts. I thought he was hot in the photo, then he was better through the window, but up close, he's otherworldly.

"Hi." Noah's throaty voice floats around me. "You must be Kristin."

Instead of speaking, I stand here with my mouth hanging open. Some small sounds that could be words escape, but they aren't coherent.

Kill me now.

"Noah, this is my best friend, Kristin. Who we told you about." Heather elbows me.

"Yes. Me. Hi. Kristin. I. You. Hi."

Smooth. Someone should video this because I'm sure it's highly entertaining.

"Right." Noah flashes a blinding smile. "I hear you're a reporter?"

*Okay, Kristin, you have to speak in more than one-word increments or grunting noises.*

I grab Heather's glass she just poured and hope it'll act as a talisman. "Yes, for a small blog, but I'm that. A reporter. For a blog. I write."

And a bumbling idiot.

Noah's green eyes are filled with humor. He moves a little closer and places his hand on top of mine. "Eli filled me in a little. I'm happy I came."

I'm pretty sure I just came. At least we're all coming.

"Me, too."

His lips turn up as his eyes rake my body. "See you out there." He winks and walks back out.

My ovaries have officially disintegrated.

I turn back to Heather, who bursts out into a fit of laughter. "Oh, that was epic. You all said I was starstruck when I met Eli? You should've seen that!" Heather continues to laugh at my expense. "Yes. Me. Um. Blog. Er—" She mocks.

"Shut up." I laugh—because, really, what else can I do—and bump her hip before moving around the bar and grabbing a glass. "Now, pour me a shot before I drink straight from the bottle."

There's only one way to get through tonight.

Alcohol.

Lots of Alcohol.

# Protected

## A Masters and Mercenaries Novella
### By Lexi Blake
### Coming July 31, 2017

From *New York Times* and *USA Today* bestselling author Lexi Blake comes a new story in her Masters and Mercenaries series…

A second chance at first love

Years before, Wade Rycroft fell in love with Geneva Harris, the smartest girl in his class. The rodeo star and the shy academic made for an odd pair but their chemistry was undeniable. They made plans to get married after high school but when Genny left him standing in the rain, he joined the Army and vowed to leave that life behind. Genny married the town's golden boy, and Wade knew that he couldn't go home again.

Could become the promise of a lifetime

Fifteen years later, Wade returns to his Texas hometown for his brother's wedding and walks into a storm of scandal. Genny's marriage has dissolved and the town has turned against her. But when someone tries to kill his old love, Wade can't refuse to help her. In his years after the Army, he's found his place in the world. His job at McKay-Taggart keeps him happy and busy but something is missing. When he takes the job watching over Genny, he realizes what it is.

As danger presses in, Wade must decide if he can forgive past sins or let the woman of his dreams walk into a nightmare….

\*\*Every 1001 Dark Nights novella is a standalone story. For new readers, it's an introduction to an author's world. And for fans, it's a bonus book in the author's series. We hope you'll enjoy each one as much as we do.\*\*

# On behalf of 1001 Dark Nights,

Liz Berry and M.J. Rose would like to thank ~

Steve Berry
Doug Scofield
Kim Guidroz
Jillian Stein
InkSlinger PR
Dan Slater
Asha Hossain
Chris Graham
Fedora Chen
Kasi Alexander
Jessica Johns
Dylan Stockton
Richard Blake
BookTrib After Dark
and Simon Lipskar